EVERYTHING THAT MOVES

BY BUDD SCHULBERG

Fiction
What Makes Sammy Run?
The Harder They Fall
The Disenchanted
Waterfront
Some Faces in the Crowd
Sanctuary V
Non-fiction
Loser and Still Champion: Muhammad Ali
The Four Seasons of Success
Swan Watch (with Geraldine Brooks)
Plays and Screenplays
A Face in the Crowd
    (Screenplay, with introduction by Elia Kazan)
Across the Everglades (Screenplay, with introduction)
The Disenchanted (Play, with Harvey Breit)
What Makes Sammy Run?
    (Musical, libretto with Stuart Schulberg)
On the Waterfront (with afterward)
Anthology
From the Ashes—Voices of Watts
    (edited, with an introduction)

EVERYTHING THAT MOVES

by
BUDD SCHULBERG

DOUBLEDAY & COMPANY, INC.
GARDEN CITY, NEW YORK
1980

Acknowledgment:
To Stan Silverman, for invaluable editorial assistance and persistence from Dartmouth *Jack o' Lantern* days onward.

ISBN: 0-385-00521-0
Library of Congress Catalog Card Number 79-7809
Copyright © 1980 by Budd Schulberg
Printed in the United States of America
First Edition

For Gerry,
and for Bobby

. . . marching on.

And for Sam,
honest trade unionist
who ran for his life.

EVERYTHING
THAT MOVES

1

A bowling ball goes thundering down the alley. It smashes the pins for a ten-strike!

The triumphant bowler is a brawny, rough-hewn man in his early thirties whose body and personality exude power, energy, and animal spirit. This is Joey Hopper. He wears a bowling-team jacket with HENDERSON OILERS—COUNTY CHAMPS embroidered in gold.

Joey lets out a caveman cry of triumph. In the final frame of the final round, his splintering strike has won the tournament. A scorer circles in chalk the winning-team total on the large blackboard headed HENDERSON COUNTY INDUSTRIAL LEAGUE.

Among the teammates clustering around to congratulate Joey is Art Nielsen, only a year older but less solidly built, made of gentler, more delicate stuff. Another in the happy crush is Art's older brother, Pinky, a man in his middle forties, small, wiry, almost bald, the likable clown of the team. On hand to give Joey a victory hug

are the Strega sisters, Paula and Edna, attractive Polish
mail-room workers, wearing HENDERSON OILERS windbreakers and pleated short skirts.

Paula, the younger, is whistle-bait, confident of her
attractions, animated, outgoing, the cheerleader of the
bowling team and the belle of Muscle Hollow, the working-class district on the wrong side of the Hendersonville
tracks. Edna is a few years older, almost as pretty, but in
a quieter, more reserved way.

In a brief ceremony, a handsome silver-plated bowling trophy is presented to Joey Hopper by George
Henderson, Sr., a white-haired, distinguished-looking,
rather old-fashioned gentleman in his late sixties.

"The members of the far-flung Henderson family
have always been known for giving their all, whether in
the oil fields, behind the wheels of our trucking fleet, or
in the bowling lanes, where you Henderson boys have
now come through again to retain the county cham-
pionship. That's the real Henderson spirit!"

By family tradition, George Henderson owns, or
feels he owns, Hendersonville, Henderson County, and all
its considerable resources. He is a power both industrially
and politically throughout the entire northern section of
the state. At his side is a dark, overweight, self-indulgent,
impeccably dressed man in his late thirties; dissipation
has added years to his age: George Henderson III, sole
heir to the Henderson fortune.

Joey, Art and Pinky Nielsen, the Strega sisters, and
the others look around with stifled yawns as Henderson,
Sr., goes on—and on. Even corpulent George the Third,
as he is referred to in Muscle Hollow, looks bored, but

something about his brooding stance makes his presence felt.

Paula Strega calls for an *allebeevo* for Joey Hopper. Saucy in her abbreviated costume, she leads the cheer, ending with "H-O-P—P-E-R—HOPPER, HOPPER—Rah Rah Rah!" climaxed by an eye-catching cartwheel that twirls her almost into Joey's arms. He lifts her easily off her feet and swings her around, while everyone laughs appreciatively. Art Nielsen is a shade less appreciative than the others.

Henderson, Sr., glances at his watch and announces it is time they must be off—Governor Thayne Winslow is coming to dinner.

"Thank a lot for stopping by, sir," says Pinky Nielsen.

"My duty and my pleasure."

"Say good night to Mr. Henderson," Pinky orders his fifteen-year-old son, Tommy.

The younger Henderson bows ironically. "Good night, gentlemen." Tough, self-contained Tommy Nielsen mutters under his breath, "George the Third."

It is time for the men to get into their work clothes for the night run that services the gas stations along the route to Capital City. Art Nielsen pecks Paula Strega on the cheek; he should be back in time to take her to the Employees Council dance tomorrow evening.

Sara Nielsen wishes her husband, Pinky, a nice run. His favorite pot roast will be awaiting his return.

The oil trucks are long, shiny, aluminum tanks that flash through the darkness on their midnight run across the state. They are prominently marked "Henderson & Son." On the back the word FLAMMABLE is clearly seen—along with SAFETY FIRST.

Joey Hopper is driving with Pinky Nielsen at his side. Art Nielsen's partner is an older man, whose nickname, for good reason, is Deacon. Just behind them is a fresh kid out of high school, Billy Kasco, whose driving mate is a heavy-set Polish immigrant, "Porky," short for Porcovich.

To break the monotony of the long drive, Billy Kasco swings out and tries to pass Joey in the lead tanker. The two streamlined giants race neck and neck for a few tense moments. Then Billy pulls ahead. Joey's reaction is to gun his motor. As the winningest man in Muscle Hollow, he's a born front-runner. Pinky Nielsen, wiser, more settled, tells him to take it easy—these are high-octane tanks they're pushing, not go-carts. But Joey is going to "teach that smart-ass a lesson." "I'll get 'im on the straightaway just over the hill."

The two trucks race up the hill with Art Nielsen driving more cautiously behind. As they start down, Joey's tanker gets rolling too fast and Pinky urges him to hit the brakes. Joey tries and finds they aren't holding. Out of control, the tanker gathers speed.

At the foot of the long hill is the main street of the next town. Joey twists the wheel back and forth to try to stem his momentum. The tanker catapults across a narrow bridge into town. To avoid pedestrians and cars in this rural shopping center, Joey veers to the left, over the curb, and into the town square, which is dominated by a life-size bronze statue on a high cement base.

As the tanker careers crazily through hedges and over park benches, Joey shouts to the terrified Pinky, "Jump, jump!" Pinky tries his door. It's jammed. "Jump!" Joey shouts once more as he throws open his own door and manages to leap free.

Joey rolls over a few times athletically and finally rights himself with bruises and scratches, the driverless truck smashes into the base of the statue and flips over violently on the driver's side. Tilted precariously in the air, Pinky is frantically working the jammed door as his brother Art and the other drivers run toward the wreck.

"I told 'im to jump!" Joey shouts.

"Come on, we gotta get 'im outta there!" Art shouts back.

But as the drivers run toward the tanker, a violent explosion rocks it, and it bursts into flame. Driven back, Art, Joey, and the others watch helplessly as the truck is consumed in blistering petroleum fire. Art turns his head away as the cab is lost in angry blue flame. In the rear the printed SAFETY FIRST is searing off.

Art and Joey inch forward, past the statue, as close to the blazing tanker as they dare. The statue memorializes Colonel George Baxter Henderson, pioneer, first judge of the territory, and founder of the Henderson fortune that now rules this part of the state. Looking down from his pedestal, the colonel is an impressive figure whose right arm extends imperiously over the wreckage.

"The power brakes was out," Joey says. "And the door jammed. Pinky never had a chance."

"I heard him bitch about that two days ago," Billy Kasco says.

"It's the goddamn Hendersons' fault," Joey shouts over the roar of the fire. "The rig was in no condition to run."

Art Nielsen looks angrily at the Henderson statue rising above them. "Look at 'im standing up there. Nothing ever knocks *them* down. You think they give a damn about Pinky?"

He presses his hands against his face and rocks back and forth, moaning. Joey puts an arm around his shoulder.

"He never had no protection. Now we gotta do somethin' for the family. C'mon, Art. We gotta hang tough."

*N*ext morning Joey Hopper and Art Nielsen lead a dele-gation of petroleum drivers to the executive offices of Henderson & Son in the Henderson Bank Building. A dignified secretary tells them Mr. Henderson is in confer-ence. And he is leaving right after lunch for a Board meeting in Capital City. Perhaps they could call again to-morrow.

Art is asking what time tomorrow, when Joey, the activist, the muscle boy of Muscle Hollow, makes up his mind. "The hell with this," he says. He hitches up his blue jeans and heads for the sacrosanct door of Mr. Hen-derson's private office. Several harried secretaries and clerks jump up to restrain him. They could as easily re-strain a charging bull. He kicks at the door and bangs it open. Almost hypnotized by his bravado, Art and the other drivers follow him in.

It is a large, old-fashioned, gracious office with a sense of tradition. Behind the elder Henderson's desk is an oil portrait of his father, the colonel. With the senior Henderson is his son George and the chief accountant, a parchment-faced company retainer, Henry Nettles.

George Henderson, Sr., is outraged. "In my thirty-one years as president of this company I have never seen such insubordination!"

"Well, you gotta start sometime, Buster," Joey threatens.

"Buster!" The old autocrat tries to control himself. No one has ever dared address him by any nickname, much less "Buster."

"You may be called worse'n that before we get through with ya, *Buster!*"

The younger Henderson rather enjoys seeing his politely dictatorial father put in his place. Power excites him. He has been spoiled, bored, smothered by respectability; his position in the family empire is static, unchallenging, taken for granted by his entire circle and by himself. So, still silent, he watches with deep interest as this crude, bellicose truck driver has it out with his father.

Henderson, Sr., is saying he assumes he knows what the drivers have come for, to discuss the unfortunate accident: He will see them on his return to Hendersonville tomorrow afternoon.

"Don't give us no runaround," Joey shouts. "Pinky Nielson is dead, he left a wife and three kids. What we wanna know is, what're ya gonna do about it?"

"I am deeply sorry," Henderson, Sr., says to Art Nielsen. "I realize your brother's passing is a painful loss."

"Painful loss, hell," Joey keeps up the attack. "It's your lousy truck killed 'im. Oh, sure, you'll put up fifty bucks for a bowling trophy—big deal—but you're too chintzy to keep ya rigs in shape!"

Henderson, Sr., reminds Joey that the agreement with the Henderson Employees Council only calls for a monthly checkup of the rigs. The day-to-day responsibility lies with the individual drivers.

Art Nielsen speaks up in a different tone from Joey. "Sir, if I may say so, the Employees Council is a company union. Pinky spoke for a lot of the boys who didn't think it was giving us adequate protection."

"Yes, I know you Nielsens and your radical notions," the elder Henderson says. "Had to talk to your father quite sharply a number of times. I'm for fair play, decent treatment for my workers—after all, I built them a recreation hall. But I swore to Colonel Henderson"—he nods toward the oil painting—"there never would be a union in Henderson County. As long as I am president of the company, there never will be."

Art, thinking carefully, says calmly that they have not come to ask recognition for an outside union. But his brother's tragedy does point up the need for stronger rank-and-file representation on the Employees Council and a new contract with more safeguards for dangerous work.

"Don't you think Henderson & Son wants to guard against accidents?" Henderson argues. "After all, we lost a twenty thousand-dollar piece of equipment."

"Ya breakin' my heart with your lousy twenty G's," Joey Hopper says. "After we get finished with Pinky's funeral, maybe we oughta hold a funeral for ya fuckin' truck!"

During this face-off, George III has been writing out a check. Now he speaks up for the first time. While he agrees with his father that the company was not responsible for the unfortunate accident and that Joey was possibly remiss in not checking the brakes before the run—

"The hell I was," Joey breaks in. "They're Henderson brakes. You own the fuckin' trucks—"

—Still, the younger Henderson continues, out of the goodness of his heart he would like to do something for the bereaved family. "Here's my personal check for five hundred dollars."

Joey throws it back. "Keep your lousy check, we'll handle this our own way."

The delegation heads for the door. Then Art Nielsen turns back and picks up the check. "Mr. Henderson, don't think you're buying us off with this. But your Employees Council death benefits are pretty inadequate. My sister-in-law can use this."

"Okay," Joey says grudgingly. "Maybe it will start the ball rollin'."

The drivers exit. Henderson, Sr., is livid. He knows these Nielsens. The father came over from the old country with a lot of Scandinavian socialistic ideas. And this Hopper fellow is a hothead, a roughneck who doesn't know his place. The father was a loud-mouthed drunk who used to sell bootleg booze to the other drivers. And there's an older brother in prison for armed robbery. None of the Hoppers were worth a hoot. Joey Hopper should have been fired months ago.

"I'd go easy, Father," George cautions. "Joey Hopper is a strongboy, the rough-and-tumble champ of Muscle Hollow. The other drivers may not love him, but they admire his muscle and his readiness to use it. I think we should walk soft until we see what develops. Things are liable to be pretty hot in Hendersonsville the next few days."

Several hundred petroleum drivers, some with their wives, attend the funeral for Pinky Nielsen. After the last words are spoken over the grave and men slowly turn away, Art Nielsen, with Joey at his side, summons the drivers to a meeting in the recreation center in half an hour.

Sobered and silent, the drivers crowd into Henderson Hall. Art's speech is brief and quiet but to the point. "If my brother's death has any meaning, it's to remind us of the evils of the open shop in Hendersonville. Like our father, he always dreamed of organizing a real union. Now it's time to start. The most fitting memorial to Pinky Nielsen is to organize our own Petroleum Drivers Local."

Most of the men shout their approval. But a few old-timers, backers of the company's Employees Council, resist. "Why don't we first try to get what we want through the Council?" asks one old driver.

"To hell with the fink Employees Council!" Joey Hopper shouts.

"That doesn't answer my question," says the elderly driver.

"Well, maybe this will," says Joey. He grabs the company-union supporter, hits him hard on the jaw, and knocks him down. "Are there any other questions?" Joey asks.

Some of the drivers laugh, but rather uneasily. Art Nielsen hurries over and lifts the fallen driver to his feet, at the same time admonishing his friend. "Maybe we don't all agree, Joey, but he's got a right to have his say. Sometimes I wish you'd use your brains a little more and your muscle a little less."

"He'll live," Joey says. "Let's get this local on the road."

Art picks up the thread of the meeting. Since the sentiment for unionism seems to be running strong, he will call for a voice vote. "All those in favor of constituting ourselves Independent Petroleum Drivers Local Number One—?" With some scattered exceptions, the shout of approval is overwhelming. Now they can proceed to vote for president. Most of the members start chanting, "Art Nielsen . . . Art Nielsen . . ." Benign Deac Johnson rises to nominate him. "The Nielsens have always been the trade-union champions of Hendersonville. With the passing of his older brother, Art is the logical candidate for president."

The majority cheer and stamp their feet, but Art silences them, thanks them for their loyalty, and declines the job. He says the fight against the traditional Henderson Company open shop isn't going to be a polite debate, but a war. For this he thinks the natural leader is the fellow who led their town football team, who captained the bowling team, who talked back to the boss for the first time in Old Man Henderson's life. "I give you the champion of Muscle Hollow and the first president of Petroleum Drivers Local Number One—*Joey Hopper!*"

So Joey Hopper, thanks to Art Nielsen's modesty, wins the presidency of the infant local by acclamation.

"Mr. President," says Art. "I think the first order of business is to appoint a committee to seek recognition from Mr. Henderson."

"Who we kiddin'?" Joey shouts. "Ol' Man Henderson loves the open shop like it was some kinda holy religion. So he'll meet us and give us the runaround like he did this morning. I say we act first 'n' talk afterwards. There is only one thing Ol' Open Shop Henderson understands and that's this—"

He whirls to the nearest bowling lane, grabs a ball, and hurls it down the alley. It sends all the pins flying. "Strike!"

Some of the men, carried away by the sheer force of Joey's action, call out, "Strike is right!" Joey shouts the slogan back at them and the crowd shouts with him. Only Art Nielsen looks somewhat dubious. Sensing his hesitation, Joey punches his arm exuberantly. "Don't worry, Art, we'll knock their brains out."

Joey Hopper is at the witness table testifying before the Senate Select Committee on Improper Activities in Labor or Management.

Dennis L. Crawford, Jr., the chief counsel—in his mid-thirties, intense, shaggy-haired, casually dressed, built stringy-tough like a finely trained lightweight fighter—is asking Hopper how many times he has been arrested.

Joey's answer is like a stiff jab and a straight right: "I don't know, I never bothered to count. All I know is, poor kids get arrested a helluva lot more than rich kids."

Crawford glances over the heads of the audience to his wife, Jan, in one of the back rows. Her mop of reddish-brown hair, outdoor complexion, and athletic figure make her seem prettier than she really is. There is instant, supportive communication between them. Then young Crawford picks up the line of questioning:

"Well, Mr. Hopper, could you make an educated guess? Five arrests? Ten? One hundred and ten?"

Joey shrugs. "In the first place, it's a loaded question. Everybody knows that ninety-nine times out of a hundred the cops are on the side of the bosses."

The chairman, tall, balding, straitlaced Senator Justin McAllen, reminds Joey that he is here to answer questions, not to make political speeches.

"Okay, sure I been arrested, as a fighter for workers' rights." Joey holds his ground. "Show me a real labor leader who ain't been arrested, from John L. Lewis . . ."

"Mr. Hopper," the chairman says, "The Mine Workers are not under investigation here. The Interna-

*tional Brotherhood of Haulers and Truckers is. Now, is it
possible you don't remember the first time you were
arrested?"*

"It was shortly after you called that strike at Henderson & Son, wasn't it, Mr. Hopper?" Crawford suggests.

The Henderson strike is in progress, with Joey Hopper
commanding the picket line. Placards proclaim "Henderson & Son UNFAIR to Petroleum Drivers Local No. 1."
Another placard shows Henderson, prominently labeled
"Open Shop," hanging from a crude gallows.

The pickets are holding a narrow bridge over a
small, turbulent river, on the main road into Hendersonville. A scab Henderson petroleum truck approaches.
Joey shouts to his men, "Here they come, fellers!" The
strikers deliberately stand shoulder to shoulder athwart
the bridge. The frightened driver blows his horn and
threatens to run the men down. Joey, a blue-jeaned Napoleon, exhorts them to hold their ground. "He'll chicken
—he don't have the guts to run over us." Joey gives force
to his words by actually advancing toward the oncoming

truck. At the last moment the driver does panic, jams on his brakes, and skids to a stop. Joey jumps to the step and pulls the terrified driver out of his cab.

"Fuckin' scab—"

"Give 'im to us, we'll work 'im over," says Billy Kasco.

"I've got a better idea," Joey says. He drags the driver to the railing of the bridge, picks him up bodily, holds him by his legs over the swiftly moving river, and threatens to drop him unless he promises to stay away from Henderson trucks. Art Nielsen runs up, horrified by these tactics, and tells Joey to pull the man back to safety. Joey complies because Nielsen is perhaps the one man in the world he respects. But he blusters, "What gives with you, Art? Ya want to win the strike, don't ya?"

"Sure, Joey, but not this way."

"There's only win or lose," Joey says. "Never nothin' in between."

The exchange is punctuated by a rifle shot. Another of Joey's boys has ambushed a second petroleum truck coming up behind the first and has fired into its tires.

"Joey, who told 'em they could use guns?" Art protests. "I want to win the strike just as bad as you do, but I want to win it legit."

"First let's win it, then let's worry about legit," Joey says.

Suddenly some of the pickets look off and shout, "Cops! Here come the cops!"

About twenty Hendersonville police officers, racing up in squad cars, jump out with clubs swinging and swarm into the pickets. There is a furious free-for-all, in which Joey more than holds his own. A burly cop swings at him, but Joey ducks agilely, grabs the nightstick from the surprised officer, and fells him with it. But then three others close in on Joey and finally overpower him.

At a witness table facing the Senate Committee dais is George Henderson III. His posture reflects the contempt he revealed when his father was presenting the trophy to Joey Hopper in the recreation center. "Mr. Henderson," Dennis Crawford is asking, "would you state your position at the time of the Petroleum Drivers' strike against your company?"

"I was the vice-president of Henderson & Son, in charge of the Trucking Division."

"And in that capacity one would expect you to be strongly opposed to the violence perpetrated by Joey Hopper against your equipment and loyal drivers?"

"That's a complex question, Mr. Chief Counsel."

"And your own relations with Mr. Hopper, were they not complex, Mr. Henderson? In fact, on the basis of the sworn testimony of Sheriff Cliff Hollis of Hendersonville, 'complex' might be a rather charitable term for your intervention on behalf of Mr. Hopper—is that not so, Mr. Henderson?"

Calmly George Henderson studies his adversaries: the scrappy, young Crawford, and the staff behind him: Dave Edelman, the chunky ex-football player from Columbia with a taste for cheap cigars; Phil Mahoney, a quiet, pipe-smoking Virginian; Charley Walker, a tough-minded black intellectual who went to Dartmouth with Crawford; and Sal Santoro, the senior member of this

*youthful team, a paunchy accountant of fifty who wears
thick glasses.*

*Henderson's attitude is that he is doing them a favor
by answering their questions. "Mr. Crawford, since you
and your intrepid investigators seem to have made a
rather thorough study of my activities and relationships, I
believe you know that I am a great admirer of Nietzsche
and Spengler. I do not hold with the primitive ideologies
—capitalism, trade unionism, socialism. I believe in the
dynamics of the power principle. . . ."*

*The senator-chairman cuts in dryly: "Suppose, in-
stead of this interesting if irrelevant lecture on the dark
philosophies, you get down to earth by telling this Committee exactly what you did when Mr. Hopper was first
arrested—wouldn't that save us all a great deal of time,
Mr. Henderson?"*

Outside the offices of Henderson & Son, a torchlight
parade is demanding freedom for Joey Hopper. Placards are carried by Art Nielsen, Deac Johnson, Porky
Porcovich, Billy Kasco, the vivacious Paula Strega, Edna,
Sara Nielsen, and young Tommy.

There are taunting effigies of Old Man Henderson and banners demanding recognition of the Petroleum Drivers Local. Paula, in her fetching Henderson Oilers' cheerleader costume, leads the chanting: "We want Joey —we want a union—we want Joey—we want a union—"

Upstairs with the harassed senior Henderson is a group of his Board members, including the Mayor, several company lawyers who have come up from Capital City for the emergency, and the ever-watchful George Henderson III.

Looking out the window at the rowdy demonstration, Henderson, Sr., becomes apoplectic. "This isn't a strike, Mr. Mayor, it's downright anarchy. They've set fire to our refinery, overturned our trucks, injured our drivers! We're virtual prisoners here in our own building. I demand that you go down and break up that riot—if you have to deputize every able-bodied man in Hendersonville."

Henderson's handpicked Mayor is shaken and miserable. "Chief Hollis has already deputized more than fifty men, Mr. Henderson. It's no use, we're powerless to stop them."

"Then I am going to Governor Winslow," Henderson decides. "It's time he sent in the State Troopers—or the National Guard."

Outside, the fury of the strikers is mounting. An oversize effigy of Henderson is set on fire. Henderson, Sr., can see this clearly from his office window while his secretary is putting through a call to the Governor.

"After all, I am not on the State Committee of the party for nothing," Henderson insists. "I helped put

Thayne Winslow in the Governor's chair. He's going to
have to do something for us."

"Winslow is running for reelection next month," Henderson's son says matter-of-factly.

"What does that mean?" his father demands.

"He isn't a devout conservative like you, sir," George
says. "He's a politician. You know what Nietzsche said
about politicians."

"I am not interested in Nietzsche!" his father explodes. "I'm interested in forcing these Bolsheviks to their
senses."

"I have the Governor for you," his secretary says.

From the Governor's mansion, the impressive, white-
haired Thayne Winslow tells his old supporter he is most
regretful, but he is in a fight for his political life. He has
an antilabor record and the powerful IBHT is after his
scalp.

"But, Governor, this so-called union up here has
nothing to do with the IBHT," Henderson argues. "It's a
fly-by-night, wildcat outfit led by a troublemaker who is a
menace to society. A flying squad of State Troopers or
one company of the National Guard could wipe them out
in twenty minutes."

"I can't take the chance," the Governor answers. "If I
send them in with bayonets and they break the strike for
you, I lose the election. Of course, once I am reelected—"

"That will be too late," Henderson says. "I'm losing
fifty thousand dollars a day. It's got to be solved tonight.
Damn it all, Thayne, you ran on the right-to-work issue.
Doesn't anybody have any principles any more?"

He hangs up, crushed. His son smiles sardonically.

"Principles, Father? You amuse me. The very word is a nineteenth-century illusion. The real world is made up of tactics, strategies. The reactionary is dead—long live the actionary."

His father asks in a tired voice, "What would you do? Right now? If you sat in the president's chair?"

"I'd say we're licked. I'd say, Joey Hopper, you win—and then make the best deal I could."

The elder Henderson is shocked. "Never. Not as long as I am president of Henderson & Son. Your grandfather founded this business and I developed it. No union upstart will ever tell us how to run it!"

George shrugs. Outside, the clamor is crescendoing. Like a cornered king fighting against abdication, Henderson orders his son: "Go tell Chief Hollis to arrest the ringleaders. Use fire hoses if he has to—or tear gas. There has got to be law and order in Hendersonville!"

George Henderson finds Chief Hollis in his radio car in the parking lot. But he doesn't give the chief his father's instructions. Instead, claiming to be speaking for the company, he tells the officer he wants to be driven down to the jail to release Joey Hopper.

Joey is flabbergasted when Chief Hollis himself unlocks his cell and tells him he can thank the Hendersons for his freedom. His shirt torn, his face bruised from picket-line battles, Joey comes out to meet George Henderson III with wary curiosity.

"What's the pitch? You Hendersons goin' soft or somethin'?"

"Believe me, there's method in my madness," George says smoothly. "You and I are going to be friends."

"Look, I got no time for riddles. I got to get back to my guys." Joey hurries out.

In the office of Henderson, Sr., an emergency midnight Board meeting has been called with some eight or ten in attendance, including the Mayor, the head counsel from Capital City, and the brooding, self-satisfied George.

Henderson, Sr., says he has summoned them to face an intolerable situation. His own son has countermanded his orders. Joey Hopper's release has led to even more intense strike violence. Drastic steps will have to be taken if Henderson & Son is to maintain its seventy-five-year-old policy of freedom from labor-union dictation.

After an uneasy silence, Mr. Sawyer, the chief legal adviser, finds his voice. It is painful for him to disagree with a man he respects as much as Mr. Henderson, but he is forced to express his belief that young George acted wisely. The jailing of Joey Hopper had served only to incite the strikers further. Without the support of the Governor, the situation has become untenable.

Chief accountant Henry Nettles adds his view. The strike has already cost them $300,000. A continuing deadlock would leave the company at the mercy of its competitors, if not bring it down in total ruin.

The Mayor agrees. In fact, the entire Board of Directors is swinging over to George's side against the autocrat who has ruled this empire so long. But it is not in the elder Henderson's nature to back down to opposition. As long as he is president, he insists, he will never recognize this union, or any union.

"Then," says George with the quiet confidence that has been growing in him, "perhaps the solution to our problem is that I assume the presidency—you've been working far too hard for a man your age anyway, Father. It might be better for your health if you were to step up to Chairman of the Board and let me handle the immediate practical problems."

"There is nothing wrong with my health," the senior Henderson storms. "At sixty-nine I am still shooting golf in the upper eighties!"

But the other members of the Board agree with George. They urge the old man to make way for his son. "These are changing times," Sawyer suggests. "Perhaps a younger, more flexible man is better able to cope with them."

Reluctantly Henderson, Sr., says he will bow to their judgment. George, full of his new sense of power, tells the Mayor, "Send word to Hopper and Nielsen that I am ready to meet with them here at nine in the morning to work out a contract between Henderson & Son and Petroleum Drivers Local Number One."

As the meeting breaks up, the defeated elder Henderson turns to his son. "I'm not sure I understand this world any more."

"Maybe I do," George says.

"A union contract." The retiring president shakes his head. "This could be the end of Henderson & Son."

"On the contrary, Father." George smiles. "I see this as the beginning—the greatest period of expansion in our history."

"Colonel Henderson would roll over in his grave," the older man says sadly.

"The exercise might do him good."

Henderson, Sr., frowns and reaches for his velvet-lapelled overcoat, his homburg, and his cane. "Good night, gentlemen," and to his son he adds coldly, "And good night to you, Mr. President."

In a crude, barnlike hall, the petroleum drivers of Hendersonville and their wives and girl friends are holding a victory beer bust. Art Nielsen, most of the other drivers, and, of course, the Strega sisters are dressed for the occasion in their Sunday best. But Joey Hopper, ever the roughneck even in victory, wears an open-neck shirt and clean blue jeans. He also sports a small adhesive tape over one eye, a trophy of his picket-line captaincy.

Joey mounts a chair, hollers for silence, and waves a batch of papers over his head like a flag. "Here it is, boys and gals—the first union contract in the history of Hendersonville!"

The celebrants cheer lustily. Joey shouts out the triumphant clauses. "A thirty-cent-an-hour raise! Overtime after forty-three hours!" In an aside he adds, "We'll get that down to forty next time around"—and everybody laughs. At this moment he can do no wrong. Paula Strega, standing beside him to steady the chair, smiles up at him in open, inviting admiration. Joey hurries on to call out other union gains: "Two men to a cab on any run over eight hours. And female members, office workers and checkers, to be paid a minimum of three dollars an hour—you know what this means, gang? A Magna Charta putting an end to feudalism in Hendersonville!"

Some of the boys whistle at the fancy language and Joey answers them with an engaging grin. "I don't know exactly what all them words mean, but Art Nielsen, our well-known high-school graduate, told me to say it."

Joey gets his laugh and calls out, "And now beer for everybody in the house. Long live Local 101!" As he jumps down from the chair, Paula throws her arms around him. "Joey, you were terrific. I'm so proud of you I could kiss you."

"Well, what's stoppin' ya?" Joey laughs, grabs her, and kisses her hard on the mouth. Drawn to his strength, she responds, and for a moment or two they are oblivious of the crowd milling around them. Then Art Nielsen approaches, his presence reminding Paula that she is supposed to be "his" girl. She draws away from Joey, allowing Art to put his arm through hers, familiarly possessive.

"Joey, you're getting to be a real speechmaker," Art says. "But where do you get that 101 stuff? We're not part of any international, we're just our own independent Local Number One."

"101—I like the sound of it," Joey says. "Makes us sound bigger."

Paula and Art laugh. "What're ya gonna do with 'im?"

The three-piece do-it-yourself band strikes up a raucous polka. Joey puts his arm around Paula assertively. "Mind if we have this spin?"

Art shrugs good-naturedly. "Nothing's too good for a union brother, not even Paula."

Held in Joey's muscular embrace, Paula asks Art to go over and ask Edna to dance. She is always a little shy at parties.

Joey pulls Paula closer—the way he does everything. "Don't hold me so hard, Joey, you're hurting me. You know what they say—you don't know your own strength."

"Oh yes I do," Joey says, as he swings her strenuously into the dance.

To everyone's surprise, George Henderson III crashes the party. Art Nielsen cusses him under his breath. But Joey says, "Relax, Art, this ain't the class struggle your old man always talked about. This Henderson kid ain't a bad joe. After all, it was him who give us the foot in the door."

"Yeah, only let's not get too buddy-buddy with him,"

Art says. "There's something a little fishy about George the Third."

Henderson aproaches full of dark charm and simulated warmth. When Porky Porcovich brings him a can of beer, George says, with a flourish, "I know it's unconventional for management to drink with labor, but as the new president of Henderson & Son, I came down to congratulate the new president of the Petroleum Drivers Local. I think we can work together constructively. It's the dawn of a new day for Henderson County, a partnership of management and labor."

Most of the men applaud, but only politely.

"Boys," Joey drops it in, "there's bosses and there's bosses. Henderson Senior and Junior is like night and day. I say *this* Henderson is a fella we c'n live with."

George acknowledges this with a modest bow, does some restrained backslapping, and Joey walks him to the door.

"You're on your way now, Joey. Don't forget who started you," George says under his breath.

"What I need ta remember, I don't forget," Joey says, his tough eyes smiling.

They shake hands formally, each sensing he has found an invaluable ally. Then Joey returns to the party.

"I don't care what he says," Art greets him. "To me he's still a Henderson."

Joey taps him playfully on the jaw. "Artie, baby, you worry too much. We'll put a ring in his nose before he puts one in ours." He slips his arm around Art with rough affection. "Come on, let's go chase the Strega girls around the room for exercise."

The band strikes up another off-key but enthusiastic tune. Joey and Art start a burlesque polka together, as the beer-happy hall rings with laughter.

In the Hearing Room, still another witness is facing Chief Counsel Dennis Crawford and the Senate Committee. This is J. B. Archer, tall, gray-haired, handsome, immaculately groomed, glib, in fact eloquent in speech. "Mr. Archer," Crawford is asking, "would you state the various positions you hold in your International Union?"

"I am a vice-president of the International, a personal representative of President Reed, I am president of Joint Council Number 17, with headquarters in Capital City, also chairman of the Tri-State Conference of the IBHT, and president of Local 98."

"And you draw salaries from all these jobs?"

"No, sir, I do not. Some of these positions I fill without compensation, out of my duty to the Brotherhood."

"In other words, your own sense of proportion as a leader of labor has limited you to a salary of $52,500 a year?" Crawford asks, suppressing a smile.

J. B. Archer's answer is confident. "You have the figures in front of you and I believe that is correct."

"We also have a memorandum from the International signed by your General President, Bill Reed, showing that you are entitled to an unlimited expense account. Is that not also correct, Mr. Archer?"

"Absolutely true and I would defend it on the grounds that holding down more than a half a dozen jobs from the International to the local level, I must be constantly on the road. In a normal week I may sleep in five

widely separated cities. I think I'm entitled to every cent of my expense account."

Dennis Crawford nods. "We have a bill here from I. Magnin for three mink stoles at seven hundred and fifty dollars each—signed by you and paid by the treasurer of Joint Council 17. Would that be a legitimate union expense?"

J. B. Archer hesitates for a moment and then smiles with aplomb. "I might remind the chief counsel that our million members include not only truck drivers but some two hundred thousand ladies, office workers, checkers—"

"And your union is in the habit of donating mink stoles to female members?" Crawford asks. "I should think in that case you would be swamped with distaff applications."

The chairman raps to choke off the spectator laughter. "Seriously," Crawford continues, "can you identify the recipients of these particular mink stoles?"

"Sir, I acknowledge that this bill bears my signature, but I am, frankly, unable to recall the circumstances."

"All right," Crawford concedes. "Our Mr. Santoro has compiled an interesting list of similar purchases okayed by you, which we will go into later in the day. But first I would like to ask you some questions about Mr. Joey Hopper. Would you say that you have been more closely associated with him than have any other executives in the IBHT?"

"Well, I had the honor of bringing him into the International," J. B. Archer answers.

Chairman Justin McAllen has a tart question. "You are quite sure that is an honor?"

J. B. Archer takes the offensive. "Definitely. I am a professional labor leader. I came out of the Depression days, the old CIO fight for workers' rights, for the decency and dignity of the workingman, and I say—"

Dennis Crawford cuts in to note that Mr. Archer seems fond of falling back on his days as an officer of the CIO, but in fairness to the respectable labor movement, that is not the concern of this Committee. The record should show that the IBHT has been suspended by the AFL-CIO and that a motion for outright expulsion is coming up at the next meeting of its Executive Board.

"Sir, in my opinion, the AFL-CIO would be making a grave mistake," J. B. Archer answers. "No organization of more than a million members can be perfect, but I am proud of the accomplishments of the IBHT and no amount of harassment by the government or by the self-appointed saints of the AFL-CIO can hide the fact that we've come a long way in the relatively short time since we first heard of Joey Hopper. . . ."

In J. B. Archer's luxurious suite in the Broadmore, the best hotel in Capital City, a thriving industrial center of half a million, J.B. is winding up a conference with a group of prosperous officials of his Joint Council. Also present are his secretary, Beverly Lambert, a leggy, attractive, shopworn and shop-wise lady in her early thirties; and Allie Stotzer, the small, jaunty public-relations man and fixer for the International, who is considered quite a wheel in Washington.

J.B. is giving his staff some rapid-fire instructions—see if the milk-drivers' beefs can be straightened out without risking a strike; look into that soon-to-open shopping center and make sure they realize no deliveries will be made there until their warehousemen sign up with the IBHT . . .

"How about this situation up in Hendersonville?" a portly official asks. "This new petroleum drivers local has called a mass meeting of all the drivers in the county, from the milk-and-egg deliverers to the funeral-parlor chauffeurs."

"For thirty years we've been trying to get a foothold in Henderson County ourselves," says another wheelhorse.

"Those kids up there must have something," Allie Stotzer puts in.

"I've been watching it," J. B. Archer says. "Beverly's been keeping a file for me. I thought I'd take in their mass meeting tonight on my way to the Tri-State Conference." He turns to Beverly, "Honey, tell what's-his-name, that new business agent—"

"Mooney," she says.

"Right, to have the car ready for us in half an hour. See you in D.C. Friday, Allie. And keep banging those drums for Bill Reed. I'm afraid he's going to need them."

10

*T*he unprecedented Henderson County drivers' mass
meeting is being held in a sports arena, its platform decorated with flags and slogans. The place is jammed,
with many of the drivers in their uniforms: milkmen,
bakery deliverers, over-the-road truckers, taxi drivers,
beer and soft-drink deliverers, garbage-disposal drivers,
hearse drivers. Girl ushers, clad in eye-catching home-
made uniforms and captained by Paula and Edna, direct
latecomers to their seats.

Watching from the balcony, coolly taking it all in,
are J. B. Archer and his very personal secretary, Beverly
Lambert.

Art Nielsen is at the mike in the boxing ring in the
middle of the arena. True to his nature, he is being thorough and honest in detailing the improvements in wages,
hours, and working conditions already gained by Local
101. But this presentation is as undramatic as it is earnest.
The large audience is clearly restless. Joey Hopper, sitting in a row with Deac Johnson, Porky Porcovich, Billy
Kasco, and other rank-and-filers, can sense the meeting
slipping away from him.

He jumps up, goes to the mike, and says, "Hold it a minute, Art. Maybe the contract we got for our boys is too good for these bums." His disarming grin makes some laugh out loud and others lean forward. "Now, before Brother Nielsen wastes any more breath on you guys, let's see who's willin' ta stand up and be counted—'n' who'd rather let the bosses go on makin' patsies out of 'em. We wanna see who's really interested in crackin' the open shop in Henderson County an' who wants to sit on their *hands*—I'm just bein' polite now cuz there's ladies present—the rest of their lives."

He turns to a burly, tough-looking group sitting together. "You beer drivers, you Jack Mullins and Tony Droppo there, I know you're gonna stand up—"

They do—and are followed up by some fifty other beer-truck drivers.

Joey salutes them and turns to another bloc. "And how about you soft-drink boys? Just because the stuff you haul doesn't have a kick in it doesn't mean you can't kick about your own conditions. You're takin' home at least a buck a day less than the beer drivers, so you're suckers if you don't stand up, too."

The soft-drink drivers, about a hundred of them, join the growing group now on its feet.

"Now, there's some others of yuz, ya don't have to tell me why you're sittin' down—you milk drivers and garbage-disposal artists, you got to get up so friggin' early in the A.M., you ain't got no strength to stand up after the sun goes down."

There is a chain reaction of coarse, appreciative laughter. Joey Hopper may not be eloquent or even in-

formative, but just as he is an unbeatable street fighter, he
is equally unbeatable as a street talker. One by one he
urges the different groups to their feet—until only a
dozen or so sad-faced men in black suits are left: the
hearse drivers. "Okay, you guys who drive those fares
that can't talk back to you—our funeral-parlor pals—you
know whose funeral it's gonna be if you don't get the
same fair shake as the rest of us!"

The laughter of recognition sweeps over the crowd
and even brings smiles to the staid faces of the hearse
drivers. First one, then a second, and finally all of them
rise to join the thousand men standing and looking ex-
pectantly at Joey Hopper.

In the balcony, J. B. Archer nods knowingly at
Beverly Lambert. "This boy's got it!"

Now that Joey has them all on their feet, he
stretches out his arms to them like the leader-demagogue
he's discovering himself to be. "Attaway, fellas—now we'll
all stand together in union brotherhood in Henderson
County!"

Under his spell, the men shout back their approval—
"Attaboy, Joey!" "You tell 'em, Joe!" "We're with ya!"

Jubilantly, Joey pounds his right fist into his left
hand—a gesture he will make famous.

As the mass meeting breaks up on a high wave of optimism, the girl ushers, Paula and Edna prominent among
them, are collecting signed application cards from the
milling audience. Sara Nielsen is doing her bit, too, and
so is the fifteen-year-old Tommy, learning his trade-un-
ionism early.

Joey, high on his own histrionics, has to force his way through the congratulatory crowd, along with Art, who is quietly satisfied with the success of their meeting. Waiting for them at the end of the aisle are J. B. Archer and his smiling, hard-eyed Beverly.

Archer offers his business card. Joey and Art look at each other, impressed. An International Vice-President of the IBHT! A personal representative of F. William Reed, no less—"Honest Bill" Reed, one of the most powerful labor figures in America. J. B. Archer, smooth as the monogrammed silk shirt he wears, congratulates them on a magnificent job. Brother Nielsen's quiet, solid ground-ing in trade unionism and Brother Hopper's rough-and-ready rabble-rousing seem to make an ideal combination. On his way to the Tri-State IB Conference, J.B. says, he had to drop in and see this miracle for himself. His own professional organizers have had trouble just crossing the county line of this notorious feudal empire. Even with the vast treasury and organizing experience of the IB behind them, they had given up on Henderson country as a lost cause. How about coming over to the Chevron Room and telling him and Miss Lambert how they did it?

Joey and Art look at each other again. In their blue jeans, open shirts, and zipper windbreakers, they were dressed for a mass meeting of truck drivers, not for the snooty Chevron Room in Hendersonville's top hotel.

J. B. Archer laughs with sophisticated ease. After their upset success with Local 101 and the way they're stretching their trade-union muscles, he has a hunch they can move anywhere they wish in Henderson County without too much squawking from the bosses.

Art Nielsen and Joey Hopper feel out of place in the Chevron Room, an unusually tony restaurant for a town of twenty thousand. But here J. B. Archer is more in his element than in the working-class joints, the all-night diners, and the greasy spoons familiar to Joey, Art, and the boys on the local level. J.B. orders a gibson. Do they have Beefeater's? Fine—and what about Noilly Prat? To the resplendently uniformed waiter, he makes his little joke: "Just take the cork and make the sign of the cross over the glass." Beverly Lambert, shrewdly appraising, not oblivious of Joey Hopper's intact muscularity, will have the same. "How about you boys?" Art says he is not used to these fancy drinks. In fact, he has never even heard of a "gibson," but he'll try one.

"Count me out on the hard stuff," Joey says. "Just gimme a beer."

As they drink with a silky toast from J.B.—"To the truck drivers, God bless 'em, the cornerstone of our Republic"—the interview begins as a polished monologue. "You boys have done wonderfully, let's say miraculously— but let's face it, it's still pretty primitive unionism."

"What's so primitive?" Joey flares. "We've got recognition, ain't we?" And Art adds more quietly, "You heard the improvements we read off at the meeting?"

"Of course," J.B. mollifies them, "but unionism in today's America goes way beyond bread-and-butter, meat-and-potato contracts." They have to take a page from Reuther and Dubinsky, "the social dynamics of labor democracy."

"Social dynamics?" Joey butts in. "What's that?"

J. B. Archer laughs his smooth, professional, idealis-

tic laugh. Forgive him for the big words, he was a
teacher for a while in the WPA Depression days. "I'm
afraid I'm a frustrated professor. To spell it out, I used to
think—when the banks were flipping and the capitalists
were jumping out of windows—I used to think maybe
capitalism is a dead duck, maybe we need socialism, production for use, to solve the problem of hunger and desperate personal need in a society with a productive capacity to put not two, but three chickens in every pot.
But when I got working with the CIO, and now the
IBHT, I began to ask myself, J.B., why wait for that old
Wobbly pie in the sky? We can have health plans, dental
clinics, summer camps for the underprivileged, not under
an unlicensed capitalism, but under progressive unionism,
pushing capitalism toward a built-in welfare state."

Art and Joey look at each other, struggling to keep
up with the high-sounding verbiage.

"If you think I'm kidding, come down and see what I
am doing," J. B. Archer goes on, signaling the waiter.
"The summer camp of my own local is a model for the
whole country. Beverly, show them the pictures. Let
them see what we're doing there."

"Camp Brotherhood is a beautiful place—if you like
the country . . . and children," Beverly says.

Joey looks at her. "So what's the pitch?"

"No pitch, just the ineluctable logic of social trade
unionism," J.B. says, savoring the second round of gibsons
he has ordered for himself, Miss Lambert, and the rather
dubious Art Nielsen. "You belong with us, in the International," J.B. goes on. "What you pay out per capita, you
will get back double in services. Here's how far I am

willing to go. I'll recommend to Bill Reed and the Executive Board that you get charters for 101, 102, 103, 104, and 105—and that these five comprise a Joint Council that you can head up."

"The new locals would have to vote on their Joint Council officers," Art says. "One thing we're determined to do is run this thing democratic, that's why we started it, didn't we, Joey?"

"Sure, sure, the whole deal's gotta be democratic," Joey backs him up, drinking his beer from the bottle, to the French-cuff distaste of J. B. Archer and faintly amused interest of Beverly Lambert.

"If you boys go for it," J.B. presses, "and getting charters from the IB is an opportunity we almost never offer this quickly, I suggest you run your Joint Council office in conjunction with my Joint Council in Capital City. These five locals would be just the beginning for you. You'll have jurisdiction all the way down to the outskirts of the city itself. You'd find it a lot more efficient if the central office isn't limited to a relatively small town like Hendersonville."

"I don't know about that," Art says. "I like Hendersonville, I'm used to it here. Hell, I even know the grooves in the bowling alleys. You know what I mean."

"Sure I do—if you want to stay small-town," J.B. says patronizingly. "How about you, Joey?"

"How much is in it?"

"You mean for you, personally?"

"Well, a fella oughta know where he's goin'—in dollars and cents—before he makes his move."

"I get the picture," Beverly says. "He's Tom Sawyer,"

nodding toward Art, "and this one"—she lifts her glass to Joey—"he's Huck Finn with muscles and money in his eyes."

"As president of a small Joint Council there wouldn't be too much," J.B. explains. "Tell you what, though—I could make you a state organizer at twenty thousand dollars a year, a union car at your disposal with free gas and oil, and traveling expenses for every day out of town. The way taxes run these days, I'd say it's like a square thirty to thirty-five thousand dollars a year."

"Thirty-five thousand dollars a year! What would you do with all that money, Joey?" Art asks.

"I'd hide it," Joey laughs.

"Think it over and let me know, boys," J. B. Archer says, snapping his fingers for the check and tossing out a hundred-dollar bill to pay it. "I think I'm putting you on to something you'll never regret."

Beverly Lambert drains her gibson. "I just hope you can say the same thing for yourself, Jay."

"What do you mean, honey?"

"Never mind," Beverly says wryly. "I hardly ever say anything and I still talk too much."

Art Nielsen looks at her questioningly. Is this what the labor movement has come to? It's not quite the way his father, an old Sam Gompers man, taught him from the cradle.

Art Nielsen is continuing his testimony before the Senate Committee. Dennis Crawford is asking him: "Now, Mr. Nielsen, as one of the founders of Local 101, is it not true that you were opposed to bringing your union into the IBHT?"

Art Nielsen answers, "Well, I guess so. I thought we were doing pretty well as independents, I didn't like the idea that our dues would be raised to pay the per capita to the International and I—well, I had heard a few funny things about the president of the International."

Crawford leans forward. "Funny? You mean, Bill Reed was a humorist? Would you mind telling this Committee what you mean by 'funny,' Mr. Nielsen?"

Nielsen is embarrassed. "Well, you know . . . there were some stories going around about Bill Reed, some of that stuff your investigators were digging up—the rank and file were beginning to talk about it."

Dennis Crawford: "But in spite of that, you didn't buck Mr. Hopper on taking your members into the International?"

"No, sir, I didn't," Art answers. "After all, there are some advantages over the road if you have area unity."

"Was that your only reason, Mr. Nielsen?"

Art hesitates. This is a personal as well as a labor question. "Well, there's no getting around it, once Joey—"

"You are referring to Mr. Hopper?"

"Joey Hopper, who else? Once he gets his mind on something, wild horses can't stop him!"

11

Art Nielsen's house is a dilapidated five-room frame on the outskirts of Hendersonville, beyond suburbia, where a poor man can raise some chickens and ducks, maybe even keep a goat in the backyard. He shares this humble place with his father, his dead brother's widow, and her three children. Joey Hopper comes to the door, which is opened by Pinky's tough-minded son, Tommy.

Tommy says, "Hi, Joey. Nice going with the mass meeting."

Joey seems in a special hurry. He mutters a hasty "Thanks, kid, is Art here?"

Tommy says, "I'd ask you in, but we're watching 'The Waltons.' Ma's favorite program. Hold on a sec, I'll call him."

Art joins Joey on the weathered front porch. Joey's message is: He's thought over J.B.'s offer and decided to take it. There's a big world beyond the borders of Henderson County. A chance to do something for progress— on a bigger stage than they ever dreamed of.

"A chance to do something for Miss Lambert, too?" Art smiles.

"Aah—there's a thousand Miss Lamberts. Even if I never seen 'em, I can smell 'em."

"Well, I'm gonna miss you, Joey. Ever since the first grade we always got along real well."

"An' we always will, Artie boy. Capital City ain't that far away. You 'n' I been working real close together, 'n'—we'll be comin' back to visit every chance we get."

"We?"

"Ya, Paula and me."

"Paula?"

"It ain't easy to break this to ya, Art, but, well, Paula's in love with me—she's been crazy about me all summer, but we didn't have the heart to tell ya. She's comin' with me, Art. It's—"

"Social dynamics," Art says bitterly. "Isn't that what International Representative Vice-President J. B. Archer would call it—social dynamics?"

"Look, Artie baby, don't be—"

"I'm not," Art says on the run. "I just want to hear it from Paula."

Art hurries down the quiet road to the Stregas' house, which is even smaller and more ramshackle than his own. He rings the bell hard. Edna comes to the door. Tacitly, she lets Art know she understands why he has come. Yes, Paula is here. She's in the bedroom packing.

Feeling numb, Art follows Edna through the small, poorly furnished front room where old Pop Strega, shoes off and in his undershirt, is sucking on a beer can and watching a TV Western.

"Hullo, Arthur, hot enough for ya?" he says in his

thick Polish accent. Art goes on into the sisters' tiny back
bedroom. Paula is kneeling on the floor, folding dresses
into a cheap suitcase. When she sees him standing in the
doorway, she stops and looks up guiltily.

"So you're really going?" Half statement, half accusa-
tion.

"We should've come to you. We should've talked to
you about it," Paula says nervously.

Art shrugs, not really successful at nonchalance.
"Why? I don't own you, I just—took you to dances, things
like that." He pauses, a painful pause for both of them. "I
mean, I—never asked you to marry me."

Paula jumps at this as if for self-justification. "I know
it, Art. But Joey, he didn't ask me, he told me. Art, would
ya believe it, he's never said 'I love you'—he's never even
said I'm pretty and things like men say when they, you
know, when they want you to do something. He just says
all of a sudden—'Start packin', you're comin' to Capital
City with me.' I says, 'Joey, I can't go with ya, I mean if
we ain't married.' 'So okay,' he says, 'we'll get married.'"

She sees Art's pain and hurries to embrace him, talking the usual Dear-John-forgive-me's: "Oh, Art, I hope it
doesn't hurt you too much, you've been awfully sweet to
me, Art, I hope you'll always be . . ."

Art breaks in, unable to hide his bitterness, "Like
they say in your favorite magazine"—there's a copy of
True Romance on the floor near the suitcase—"lifelong
friends? Sure, we'll be lifelong friends, Paula. I can understand how it goes with a fella like Joey. I think everything I ever wanted, he got there ahead of me. I wanted
a new bike once so bad I could taste it—first prize in a

newsboys' contest for the most subs sold for *The Chronicle*, so who won it on the last night by one subscription? One guess: Joey Hopper. From selling papers to the bowling cups to grabbing off the prettiest kid in Muscle Hollow. He's a natural, he's the winner."

"Don't hate 'im, Art," Paula begs. "He doesn't do it to be mean."

"I know that, Paula," Art says and he means it. "He does it to be Joey Hopper."

She nods, with tears. He understands. Joey Hopper is too big for her, too big for either of them, maybe too big for anybody.

"Something tells me he's going to go awfully far, Paula. Just as far as Mr. Archer thinks. Maybe even farther."

"Maybe you can sort o' keep an eye on Edna," Paula suggests. "Take her bowling or to the movies once in a while. She's gonna be awfully lonely without me. Momma gone and Poppa beered up all the time, she's gonna feel like an orphan."

"Sure, I'll take her to the movies," Art says. "With Joey gone and you along with him, I'm—gonna feel a little like an orphan myself."

Outside, an automobile horn sounds impatiently. Tommy Nielsen, who has been playing ball with some of the other kids in the street, runs into the Strega house. "Holy cow, Paula, you ought to see what you're goin' to Capital City in—a Cadillac! A big black Caddy about a hundred feet long!" They all rush out to see this marvel— probably the first time a Cadillac has ever driven into Muscle Hollow. Joey Hopper, scrubbed, but otherwise

making no sartorial concessions to his new estate, is all
grin and muscular confidence. "Pretty nice, huh? Mr.
Archer sent it up for me."

The send-off is a festive moment, one that Muscle
Hollow will long remember. Paula is dressed in her most
elegant twenty-dollar gown. Her feelings are torn, gener-
ally sorry to leave the only home she has known since she
came from Europe as a little girl, all the familiar faces
and sights, Edna, Art, even unshaven, slovenly old Poppa.
But this is a chance to see the world.

Gathering around the shiny Cadillac are all the
neighbors, Sara Nielsen, young Tommy and his gang,
Art's father, and local drivers like Deac Johnson, Porky
Porcovich, and Billy Kasco. There is some good-natured,
hardhat kidding: "Don't let that Caddy go to your head,
Joey. . . . If us fellas didn't know ya so good, we'd think
ya sold out to them fat cats f'sure!"

Joey takes it good-naturedly. "Don't worry, fellas,
Joey Hopper knows what side his Cadillac is buttered
on."

There are cries of "Attaboy, Joe!" "God bless ya,
Jocy!" "Eat 'em bosses up alive!"

Joey reaches out a window to acknowledge the
cheers with his hard-fist-into-left-hand gesture.

Just as the Cadillac is about to drive off, George
Henderson III pulls up in his spectacular red Maserati.
Art Nielsen, his father, and other unionists edge away;
they don't fraternize with the bosses. But the younger
Henderson is all affability. He is glad he caught Joey on
his way out of town. Just wanted to wish him luck. "Inci-

dentally, I keep a suite at the Broadmore—so does the IBHT. So we should be seeing a lot of each other."

"Sure, pal, why not?" Joey calls out, and then the Cadillac drives off toward the big city with some of the kids like Tommy Nielsen jumping on the back for fun, until the big car is going too fast for safety.

Stoically, Art and Edna watch it disappear around the next corner. "Come on in, Art," she says in a monotone, "I'll make you a cup o' coffee."

12

Whenever Paula thought of marriage, she had dreamed of a family ceremony in the local Catholic church, performed by old Father Stanislaus, who had officiated at her first communion. "No time for that stuff!" Joey had vetoed a formal wedding. A quick stop at a J.P. on the way is the best he can do. Swept along, Paula swallows her disappointment and manages to smile, "I do."

Their arrival at the Broadmore—in bustling, prosperous Capital City, the commercial hub of the state—whisks them Cinderella-like into a palace world they never knew. Suddenly Paula feels nakedly poor in the dress that looked so spiffy in Hendersonville; now she is up against the sleek, smartly coiffed, expensively gowned ladies thronging the lobby. Joey is still dressed like the common truck driver he so recently has been. But, as usual, his attitude is—who gives a damn? Undaunted, he swaggers through the lobby where they are met by Beverly Lambert, attractive in a stylishly mannish Italian suit.

"On behalf of the International Brotherhood," she says with barely a hint of the cynicism she feels for everything and everybody, "welcome to the big city." She'll show them to the room Mr. Archer has reserved for them until they can find a home to rent or buy. Archer is in a meeting, up in his suite, 15-A, and he would like Joey to join him there just as soon as he's had time to unpack and clean up. On the way to the elevator, Beverly looks Paula up and down. "You'll probably want some clothes for the city. As soon as I get a few hours free, I'll take you to the shop the IB does business with, and open a charge account for you."

Once inside their hotel room, Joey kisses Paula perfunctorily. "Well, honey, we made it to the first pole."

Paula says, "I don't like that girl."

Joey laughs. "Miss Lambert? I hear they call her the favorite sister of the Brotherhood."

Paula says, "She's got awfully pretty legs for a sister an' she's got a roving eye. I could see her sort o' feelin' ya up with her eyes."

Joey laughs again. "Don't worry, Paula, I didn't come down here to score that way. I'm gonna score where it counts. Get the stuff hung up. I'll go up 'n' check in with Mr. Archer."

"Lookin' like that?"

"Why not?" Joey grins, hiking up his blue jeans. "Do
those beer bellies good to see an honest t' God workin'
stiff once in a while." He slaps her on the butt and strides
toward the door.

Joey shoulders into the elegant suite of J. B. Archer,
its bar stocked with the finest whiskeys. A group of
prosperous-looking, well-fed men have gathered here.
They could be successful businessmen, but are not as
suave as Archer: under their expensive barbershop ve-
neer, they're cruder and tougher.

J.B. introduces Joey. These are local officers, Joint
Council officers, business agents. "Make yourself at home,
Joey," J.B. says. "We're just having an informal meeting,
working out some of the points we're going to ask for at
the bargaining session with the Joint Employers Council
this afternoon."

Joey perches on the arm of a brocaded wing chair.

A burly, veteran business agent, Ned Green, is
suggesting that the phrase "come to rest" for an over-the-
road truck should mean not only back up to the platform
but also in the yard or even in the street immediately ad-
jacent to the yard or terminal.

"Just a minute, pal," Joey breaks in. "I've hauled inta
places where ya can't even park in the street outside the
terminal. So why give 'em a loophole? Why not make
'come to rest' the closest place the driver can find to the
terminal—wherever that is, in the driver's discretion?
From there on, they gotta put on a local man to drive the
peanut wagon to the platform."

The assembled union bosses look at each other. Who

is this young punk? Whoever he is, he sure'n hell knows
his trucking business.

"You see why I brought him down here?" J. B.
Archer says, like a proud father. "He may look like a muscle boy, but he's got a few brains tucked away under
those muscles."

Archer's yes-men laugh uneasily.

When the meeting breaks up, J.B. opens the door
that connects his suite with another, equally lavish,
where a covey of call-girls are sitting around drinking
and listening to Stevie Wonder on a Sony cassette player,
volume up. "Gentlemen," J.B. says with a theatrical
flourish, "some young ladies I thought you might like to
meet, especially you out-of-town boys."

"J.B.," says Ned Green, "that's one reason I like to
come to your bargaining sessions. You've always got the
best broads in the IB."

"An' that's sayin' somethin'," says another out-of-
town officer.

Ned Green notices that Joey is hanging back.
"What's the matter, Joey? This is like one big, happy family. Don't be bashful."

Joey still hangs back. "You boys go ahead. I want to
talk to J.B."

"All right, don't tease him, boys," J.B. laughs. "He's
just in from the sticks and don't forget, he's a newlywed.
Six months from now, he'll be beating you to the door of
15-B."

There is coarse laughter as these middle-aged, portly
"boys" troop in to join the girls. Joey watches them with
poker-faced disapproval, not from any sense of moral out-

rage, but because he is already sizing up his new colleagues—and finding them wanting.

J.B. watches Joey watching the "negotiating committee." Archer has weaknesses of vanity and of the flesh,
but as a trade unionist he is a seasoned veteran and he
knows he has found something very special in Joey
Hopper.

"Come on," he says, "I want to introduce you to my
tailor."

"I wore my big brother's stuff till I was eighteen,"
Joey says. "Store-bought is good enough for me."

"Didn't know you had a big brother. Where is he?"

"None of ya fuckin' business."

"You're tough," J.B. says. "I've got a lot of fellas
around me who look tough and talk tough—but you're
tough."

"Enough," Joey says. "Let's go."

In the English tailoring shop, where J. B. Archer is
obviously a favorite customer, the vice-president of the
International picks out an expensive material for Joey
and gives some Cary Grantish instructions on how it
should be cut. When Joey hears the price—$250—he whis-
tles. In Hendersonville his Sunday best set him back
$24.95. He cannot afford $250—not even on his magnificent new salary.

"Don't worry about it—be my guest," J.B. says graciously.

"Or the guest of Joint Council 17?" Joey asks impu-
dently. "That unlimited expense account?"

"We are getting a higher rate for our men than anybody in the country," J.B. says, "so don't knock it."

The obsequious tailor goes on fitting his impatient customer.

In a plush custom-shirt store, the clerk is measuring Joey for silk shirts with French cuffs. "And for the monogram," J.B. is saying, "I want a large 'H' in English script in the middle, a smaller 'J' on one side—and what's your middle name, Joey?"

"Middle name?" Joey laughs. "I'm lucky I got a first name and a last name."

"What was your father's name?"

"My old man? Tom. In Muscle Hollow they called him Tough Tom."

"I can believe it. Is he deceased?"

"Diseased—hell, he's dead!"

J.B. checks a smile. "What did he die of, Joey?"

"Every Saturday night after he come out of the mine —it was a sweet six-day-sixty-hours in them times—he'd head for Sullivan's saloon and drink up the check. One Sunday morning they found 'im in the gutter outside the joint—when it come to drinkin', he could give lessons to a fish."

"A miner," J.B. says thoughtfully. "That's good. In the image of John L. Lewis. Your father died of silicosis. Remember that, Joey, it might come in handy someday."

"Okay, okay. But what do I need the initials for? I don't need to look at my shirt to know who I am."

J.B. laughs. "Joey, you've got a natural proletarian sense of humor. It's going to make you one of the best organizers I ever had."

"To hell with that 'one of the best,'" Joey says. He gestures toward the ceiling with his thumb. "I like it on top."

13

⎯⎯⎯⎯◆⎯⎯⎯⎯

That evening Joey and Paula are dining in one of the fancier restaurants in the city. Paula shows the effects of Beverly Lambert's guiding hand. She has a new, elaborate hairdo and a new, far more becoming dress. Beverly has even taught her a few tricks about lipstick and eye shadow. Paula has always generated a strong physical appeal, but now, although self-conscious about the change, she is almost chic in a slick, big-city way. Joey is wearing a new suit and even a narrow, Ivy League tie J.B. has picked out for him. When he reaches for the sugar, Paula notices another improvement. "Joey—your fingernails, they're all pink and shiny."

Joey pulls his hands back embarrassed. "Ya, Mr. Archer made me do it. They call it a manicure. Sets ya back a buck an' a quarter 'n' ya come out lookin' like a faggot. All the union guys do it here."

"I like it," Paula says. "Honey, honest you look so handsome I could cry."

"You look okay yourself," Joey says.

"I got a permanent. From a real Frenchman who knows how to speak French. Every two weeks I come in and he touches it up. Ooh-la-la!"

"Some permanent," Joey says. "That frog better watch out or I'll ooh-la-la him right in the kisser."

"Don't worry about him, honey. I think he's a queer. Hey, let's have a drink. To our new life. It sounds just like somethin' I was reading under the dryer in *True Romance*."

"Just order one," Joey says, "an' drink for the both of us. Just because I'm wearin' a tie an' got this crap on my fingernails don't mean I ain't gonna stay in shape."

"Mr. Archer drinks," Paula argues. "Gibsons, you told me, and look how important he is. It's part of being a gentleman."

"J.B. is okay," Joey concedes, "pretty smart fella. But honey, I got news—these guys are ready to be taken. In six months or a year—"

Paula calls the waiter, "Gar-son—gar-son!"

The waiter is faintly mocking. "The lady wishes something?"

"—A gibson."

"And the gentleman?"

"Just a glass of cow juice, pal," says Joey. And then

he picks up what he started to say—"I got a crazy hunch I could run this show." Joey reaches for the celery, bites off more than a mouthful, and crunches down hard.

In the red-carpeted Hearing Room illuminated with powerful arc lights, with TV cameras recording the scene and reporters busy taking notes, Joey Hopper is under fire.

At the chairman's side, with his handful of watchful associates around him, Dennis Crawford is directing the questioning.

"Now, Mr. Hopper, when you first established yourself in the Capital City area, did the gas-station attendants come under the jurisdiction of the IBHT?"

Joey Hopper snaps his answer contemptuously: "Once I got there they did."

"Once you got there? In other words, you were inventing your own bylaws, constitution?"

"Not inventing—don't try to put words in my mouth, Denny Boy." The Committee chairman, Senator McAllen, pounds his gavel. "You will kindly address our chief counsel by his proper name, Mr. Hopper. Any discourtesy to him will be construed as a contemptuous act toward this Committee and the Congress of the United States."

"Okay, Senator," Joey answers, clearly not intimidated by the chairman's authoritative tone. "But I was not inventing, I was interpreting. If you organize the truck drivers, you've got to have the riggers and the platform men, so how about the gas that goes into the trucks?

Anything has to do with wheels—even if it ain't—isn't spelled out in the constitution—I say it belongs to me, I mean to us, the IBHT."

"But when you were getting ready to call the state-wide gas-station strike," Crawford asks, "a strike which, incidentally, was called without any record of a vote that our investigators have been able to find—isn't it true that your immediate supervisor at that time, Mr. J. B. Archer, questioned the legality, as well as the wisdom, of your unconstitutional behavior?"

Joey Hopper shakes his head. "I don't remember any such conversation with Mr. Archer."

"Mr. Hopper, we have right here a memorandum from Mr. Archer, marked State Exhibit 1293, that we would like to show you. Maybe it will refresh your memory."

The memo is passed to Joey, who looks at it poker-faced.

"Now," Crawford goes on, "perhaps you will be able to tell us what Mr. Archer felt about your illegal and un-democratic strike against ten thousand gas stations in the seventeen counties surrounding Capital City."

Joey hands back the memo. "I'm sorry, Mr. Chief Counsel Dennis Crawford, sir, it don't—doesn't happen to refresh my memory. Maybe I talked to him, maybe I didn't. It was quite a while back."

Crawford exchanges looks of exasperation with his team—Edelman, Mahoney, Walker, and Sal Santoro. "But it was your first big step toward state, interstate, and

*finally national power. Surely you would remember the
details, Mr. Hopper?"*

*Joey holds his ground. "Like I say, maybe I do, and
maybe I don't. . . ."*

14

$\mathcal{J}$oey Hopper is riding with J. B. Archer in the latter's
black Cadillac. Beverly Lambert sits between them.

"Joey, I've got to hand it to you," a self-satisfied J.B.
is saying, "you've done a beautiful job of stopping the
dairy co-op from hauling its own milk to market."

"If it moves, it belongs to us," Joey says simply.

"You've brought in twenty-five thousand new
members. First time we ever had the cabdrivers sewed up
tight."

"At a bonus of fifty cents a head, you're going to be
rich, Joey," Beverly says tartly.

"I ain't interested in money," Joey says.

"What are you interested in? You don't seem to go
for money—sex—what I call the usual human induce-
ments."

They have pulled into an old-fashioned gas station
on the outskirts of the city. Joey gestures toward a

shabby, elderly man who shuffles to the driver's window to ask, "Fill 'er up?"

"I'm gonna go after these jokers next."

"Now wait a minute, Joey," J.B. points out, "that could mean a jurisdictional hassle with the Oil and Gas Workers, CIO. I'd like to ease us back into the CIO, not push them further away."

"Tough," Joey says.

"And anyway, gas-station attendants are practically impossible to organize." With his long trade-union experience, J.B. thinks he knows what he is talking about. "Some of them, like this old coot filling my tank, are independents who own their own stations, with relatives helping out part-time. Some of them are just high-school kids picking up pocket money after school."

"Tough," Joey says again.

"Beverly, you'd better call the office," J.B. says. "I'd like to find out if we've settled that overtime problem with the hi-lo's at the terminal."

Joey gets out to let Beverly pass. "Joey, sometimes you seem to forget that Mr. Archer is still your boss. If he says lay off gas stations, lay off."

"Go make your phone call, girl," Joey says, his steel-trap mind clearly sprung. "I want to talk to that old gobbler about how many hours he works, how much he brings home. I've got an idea. . . ."

15

---

*I*n George Henderson III's suite in the Hotel Broadmore, a butler opens the door to admit Joey Hopper. George comes forward in a cashmere smoking jacket and offers Joey a drink. "Drambuie, Grand Marnier, Napoleon brandy . . . ?"

"Just gimme a Coke," Joey says.

"So your new clothes, the Cadillac, and the rest of the trimmings haven't gone to your head."

"Not in that way," Joey says pointedly.

"Of course I have been hearing about your success," George says. "In a matter of months you've become the most valuable member of Archer's team. The fullback they give the ball to when they need those few extra yards."

"I used to play fullback for the Hendersonville semi-pros," Joey says.

"I remember well," George says. "You know, I've been following your career. In fact, I could go so far as to say it's been an inspiration to me."

"Inspiration? That's a big word."

"I was ready to settle for being a ne'er-do-well,"

George explains, "you know, the decadent heir of a wealthy and powerful father. Not enough ambition to strike out for myself and nothing really to do inside the company except appear at Board meetings and vote *ja*. Then you came along, and I saw how my father was handling, or rather mishandling you, the old-fashioned open-shop way."

"It worked out pretty good," Joey says.

"A bare beginning," George says, pouring himself a Chivas straight up. "You've given me a cause, Joey Hopper, a reason for existing." He smiles. "I may even give up twelve-year-old scotch and take up barbells like you."

"What's the pitch, George?" Joey asks. "I still got some city pickup contracts I want to look over t'night."

"I thought you had lawyers for that."

"Screw the lawyers. I wanna be able to tell the lawyers."

"Bravo," says George. "That's why I find myself drawn to you, Joey. J. B. Archer, he's a quasi-socialist, a spoiled priest of the labor movement, with high ideals and low morals. My father, he believes in nineteenth-century free enterprise, Adam Smith, spirited but honest competition, and that sort of rot. You and I, we're not capitalists or socialists or reactionaries or laborites, we're —activists."

"Ya—so?"

"I'm a great admirer of Nietzsche," George says. "Read a few passages almost every night before I go to sleep. It's my Bible—I should say my anti-Bible. Nietzsche reduces all human behavior to a single drive, the will to power. Down with altruism, up with selfishism. This writer, Ayn Rand"—her book, *Atlas Shrugged,* is at hand—"says the same thing."

"You and J.B. ought to get together. Book readers. I'll give ya one minute more, George. What's the pitch?"

"I hear you're out to organize the gas stations."

"You hear good. But from where?"

"One of the switchboard girls. For an extra fifteen a week. You'll learn all those tricks and invent a few more."

"So?"

"So you and I are going to organize the gas stations together."

"Ya sure make a funny-looking union man, George."

"I'm not a union man, Joey. I'm a back scratcher. I scratch the IBHT and you scratch Henderson & Son."

Joey jumps up, excited. "I get the picture! We sign a contract with Henderson & Son and we use that as a club to beat your competitors into line. I'm ready, George!"

"A couple of details," George says quietly. "So far we're only scratching *your* back. Here's how you scratch mine. I'll sign for three dollars and a quarter an hour—if you'll hold out for three seventy-five for every other gas company in the state."

"Inside a year," Joey says, "you'll put all the little guys out of the business. In this area you'll be bigger than Standard Oil and Texaco."

"And you'll have at least twenty-five thousand new members, and probably more votes in the Tri-State Conference than J. B. Archer himself."

Joey puts out his hand. "Who's the longhair bookwriter you tout so high?"

"Nietzsche?"

"Ya—if that's Nietchee, he's thinkin' pretty good."
Joey rises to go. "You got a deal, George."

"I'll work it out on my side. We'll be in touch,"
George says, walking Joey to the door. "Oh, one more
small item . . ." He would rather not have Henderson &
Son be the first to sign the contract. His competitors
would raise too much hell in the Gas Distributors Association. But he will be the second to sign.

It is one of those rare moments when Joey is puzzled. "But there is no first."

"There will be." George reaches in his pocket casually. "Here's twenty thousand. Go buy yourself three or
four locations, incorporated in your wife's name—"

"—Her maiden name," Joey breaks in.

"For a Muscle Hollow kid who barely got through
the sixth grade!" George III throws him a little salute.

"Ya don't need lawyers to think," Joey laughs. "Ya
need lawyers ta put the thinkin' into words honest people
can't understand."

"Mr. Hopper," George bows ironically as he opens
the door, "Mr. Nietzsche would be proud of you."

"Fuck Nietchee," says Joey. "Nietchee don't own no
gas stations."

A small gas station, identified by a brand-new sign as Agerts Oil Company, is being picketed by a line from the IBHT with challenging placards. Supervised by Joey Hopper, the activity seems peaceful and friendly.

A Henderson Oil Company station is also being picketed by IBHT members and again the action is peaceful, even friendly; again a benign Joey Hopper is overseeing.

A local television reporter heralds the news that Agerts Oil Company is first to sign with the IBHT. A second newscast shows George Henderson III shaking hands with Joey Hopper: Henderson Oil is next to fall in line.

Now the IBHT flying squad is going after one of the Henderson competitors, Richwell Oil. There are twice as many pickets and they are clearly hostile and rowdy. Two teenage boys wearing high-school nylon jackets ride up on motor scooters. The picket-line leader blocks their approach. "Where you goin'?"

One of the boys says, "We work here after school."

"Are you members of the IBHT?"

The boys look at each other nonplussed. "IBHT? What's that?"

"International Brotherhood of Haulers and Truckers."

The youngsters back away, intimidated by the gathering line of beef. "But we're not truck drivers, we're only—"

The picket-line captain looks toward the curb at Joey Hopper, who merely nods. The rest is automatic. The captain and a couple of other burlies move in. One-two and the boys are smashed to the sidewalk and their scooters thrown into the street.

An older picket, looking on, says, "You sure this is right, Mr. Hopper? They're just kids. I got a son their age."

"Sixteen or sixty-six," Joey lays down the law, "it adds up—scab." Then he says to the picket captain, "Okay, I'm gonna check some other locations. Keep a tight line."

At the Senate Committee hearing, George Henderson III is back in the witness chair.

Dennis Crawford is on the scent of the curious ties between management head and labor leader. "Now, Mr. Henderson, as one of the influential industrialists in your state, increasingly influential I might add, this Committee is interested in your continuing relationship with Mr. Hopper and the IBHT. You were the first of the major gas companies of your area to sign a contract with Mr. Hopper's organization, were you not?"

George Henderson answers with a small smile. "I—er —believe we were not quite the first, possibly the second or third."

Crawford glances at a note handed to him by Dave Edelman. "Mr. Edelman, who, as you know, conducted an investigation in your area, tells me you were the first company of any size to sign with the IBHT. Actually the very first was Agerts Oil, a small company, organized on the eve of the strike."

The chairman turns to Crawford. "Counsel, have we been able to penetrate the mystery of the so-called Agerts Oil Company?"

George Henderson speaks up. "I understand it is a legitimate business operation which in no way—"

"Your statement is gratuitous, Mr. Henderson," Crawford interrupts. "I wish you were as willing to volunteer information about your own company's activities."

Henderson flushes. "I protest—as a responsible member of a distinguished—"

The chairman pounds his gavel. "The chief counsel will answer my question and then may proceed with his own."

Dave Edelman hands Crawford another note, and the chief counsel says, "Senator McAllen and members of this Committee, we are not prepared at this time to pursue a line of questioning regarding Agerts Oil. As a matter of fact, our investigators in the field have encountered considerable difficulty locating the files we wish to study —or even locating the officers of this company. At a later date we hope to call the appropriate witnesses."

Senator McAllen nods. "Proceed with your questioning of Mr. Henderson."

And Crawford does, a young man sure of his facts, though inwardly exasperated that they have a way of slipping through his fingers.

"Now, Mr. Henderson, you may cavil as to whether you were first, second, or fifth, but you were certainly the first member of the Association to sign with the IB, at a time when the Association felt that the union, and Mr. Hopper in particular, were making excessive demands. Is that not true?"

"Mr. Crawford," George III answers with a great show of assurance, "we are in a public-utility field. After all, gasoline and trucking go to the very vitals of this great country. There are times when we must think not of our selfish corporate interests, but of the public as a whole."

"And it is in that spirit that you interpreted your contract with Mr. Hopper?" Crawford asks. "A contract we intend to go into in some detail before these hearings are over—is that what you are testifying under oath, Mr. Henderson?"

"Yes, sir, I do—or rather in the interest of grammatical accuracy, I am—I certainly am."

"By all means let us keep this record accurate or at the very least grammatical," Dennis Crawford says.

Edelman, Walker, and the other investigators grin. Crawford manages to keep a straight face as he persists:

"I ask you again. Did you interpret your contract with Mr. Hopper as serving the public interest? Even in

view of the violence? I am speaking not of isolated cases, but of the very pattern of violence by which the general gas-station strike was conducted."

"Sir, I was never aware of any violence," George Henderson asserts. "I knew Joey Hopper, of course. It often was necessary for us to negotiate together. But I knew Mr. Hopper only as a law-abiding, conscientious labor leader."

The chairman says, "Thank you, Mr. Henderson. If you will consider yourself on call, I think we may wish to have you testify again later in the day." He asks the chief counsel to call the next witness.

It is Mr. Samuel J. Eichels—the old gas-station owner who serviced J. B. Archer's Cadillac when Joey Hopper was first conceiving his organizing campaign. Eichels has become more infirm, considerably more shaken, and now wears a hearing aid.

"Samuel J. Eichels, do you swear to tell the whole truth and nothing but the truth, so help you God?"

Eichels hesitates and then mumbles, "So help me God."

"Mr. Eichels," the chairman advises the frightened old man, "as you know, every witness who comes before us is entitled to counsel. Do you have counsel with you?"

"No, your honor. I come to answer the questions."

There is tittering in the hearing room and the chairman gavels for order. "Proceed, Mr. Chief Counsel."

"Mr. Eichels, what is your present occupation?"

Eichels hesitates once again. Then: "I'm a gas-station attendant."

"Would you kindly speak up, sir?"

Eichels forces his voice higher: "Gas-station attendant."

"Employed—?"

"By the Henderson Oil Company."

"Was that always your position, Mr. Eichels?"

"No, sir, I used to be what they call an independent operator."

"And would you mind telling this Committee what brought about your change in status?"

"Well, one day these fellas come up to me—"

"I'm sorry to interrupt, Mr. Eichels, but could you try to make your testimony a little more specific?"

"Well, they wanted me to join their union. I told 'em I own my own place, had my wife an' my brother-in-law fillin' in for me, and we didn't need no union."

"What happened next, Mr. Eichels?"

"Nothin', for a few days. Oh, there was a lot of telephone callin' in the middle of the night and things like that. And o' course the picket line was marchin' up and down, 'Unfair to Organized Labor.' Hell's bells, I didn't have no labor to organize, it was only me and the missus and her brother."

Crawford pushes the reluctant Eichels on. "And then . . . ?"

"Well, one night a car drove in for gas and when I pushed the valve—the next thing I knew the tank blew up in my face—my clothes was on fire—I came to in the ambulance . . . I was in the hospital better'n two months."

"And when you came out, you joined the IBHT?"

"Yes, your honor. I talked it over with the missus—

her nerves were so bad she'd start cryin' every time a car drove up—an' we thought we better sign up."

The chairman asks: "Do you think your case is typical of the independent gas-station operators in your state, Mr. Eichels?"

"Think? I know. After Mr. Hopper got through with us, there wasn't an independent from border to border. Even a lot of the smaller chains went under. Most of us sold out to Henderson Oil and went to work for him for three-twenty-five an hour. And lucky to get it."

17

Dennis Crawford drives his old convertible up the long driveway to the rambling country house in Maryland. As he gets out with his briefcase and an armful of reports—his homework for the evening—he receives an enthusiastic greeting from an ancient St. Bernard.

"That's enough, Cato. Behave yourself!"

Then a small fist catches him in the stomach. It belongs to Anthony, the seven-year-old who hits people if they call him Tony. In fact, he likes to hit people anyway.

It's a family joke that he's in training to become the Great White Hope.

His young father frees his hands and hits back at Anthony, hooking to the body, a little harder than one would expect a grown man to hit a child. But Anthony seems to relish the attack. He flails at his father with both hands and Crawford slumps to the ground.

Anthony stands over him triumphantly. "Gosh, you're slipping, Dad."

"I know," Crawford says, rising. "It's not my day. Is Mom inside?"

"Everybody's out on the back lawn, playing volleyball. I hate volleyball. It's a sissy game."

"Not the way Mommy plays it," Crawford says. Picking up his papers, he jogs around the house with Anthony to the back lawn which has been turned into an athletic center with a volleyball court, a basketball backboard, and a small swimming pool.

Jan is involved in a furious contest, teamed with four-year-old Eddie against eleven-year-old Sally and nine-year-old Tim. Eddie taps the ball to Jan, who spikes it viciously at Sally, almost knocking her down.

"Fifteen-eleven!" she calls out and shakes hands with her sweaty, pint-sized partner. "We win!"

"Well, let's make it two out of three," Tim begs.

She tosses the ball to their seven-year-old. "Substitution. Anthony going in for Mom. Mom needs to confer with Daddy on the sidelines. Also, Mom is bushed."

On the terrace as the next game starts, Jan brings

Dennis a vodka-tonic. "I had to leave early," she says. "Anything special happen?"

Crawford savors the first swallow. "Wow, this tastes great. If they hand me my head in these hearings, I c'n always get you a job as a bartender."

"Still not getting anywhere with Hopper?"

"Nowheresville."

"He's got too many lawyers."

"His own private Bar Association."

He hefts the thick reports he's brought with him. "Fourteen million words—twenty thousand man-hours— Santoro alone must have traced the endorsements on a thousand checks. And Charley Walker's legwork has been brilliant. And yet people around Joey Hopper bend the truth like a paper clip. They forget, they don't know—"

Crawford catches himself. "Every night I promise— 'No more shoptalk.' And every night I come home with a worse case of Hopperitis."

"Guess who I asked to dinner tonight?"

"Joey and Paula Hopper?"

"Very funny. The Poviches." Crawford smiles. Shirley Povich is an old friend and his favorite sportswriter.

"I should work . . ."

"At least when Shirley talks about the cheap shots they're taking at the quarterback, he's not thinking about you, he's worrying if old Billy Kilmer can get through the season."

Crawford tries to go with it. "I wonder if we shouldn't trade some of our good old over-the-hills for future draft choices and build for next year?"

Jan hands him a fresh drink. "Now that's what I call a nice, healthy, relaxing worry."

Crawford sips his drink thoughtfully. "Only I'm not coaching the Redskins. I'm trying to stop a very tough sonofabitch from taking over the whole damn country."

18

*J*ubilantly Joey Hopper and J. B. Archer are signing the new IBHT agreements with a dozen rather grim-faced gas-station-chain executives and their lawyers. Beverly Lambert is turning pages for the defeated Association members to initial. Press photographers are getting their pictures. It is a formal occasion in the banquet room of the Broadmore.

One of the signers hesitates before he adds his name. "It's a tough contract, Mr. Hopper."

"Yeah, and we're gonna enforce it, Mr. Lindsay," the expansive Joey rubs it in.

"How about Henderson?" Lindsay asks. "Are you going to enforce his, too? The word is, you boys are goin' together."

Joey flares for a moment. "Can I help it if Henderson has—what d'ya call it, J.B.?"

"Labor statesmanship—"

"Yeah, labor statesmanship," Joey picks up on it, "and signs up right away pronto—while you jokers make us sweat? That's gonna cost ya, Lindsay. You're lucky we didn't raise it another two bits."

"But you will, you will," Lindsay says wryly.

"If our members have it comin' to 'em, that's what they're gonna get," Joey says.

"Including the ones working for Henderson?" Lindsay jabs.

Joey glares at him. "Look, the debate is over. We come here ta sign a contract. Beverly, show the man where he puts his name."

Resignedly, Lindsay signs and hands the pen to the next company executive.

Under his breath to Joey, J.B. says, "Soon as this is over, I'm giving a little party up in 15-B."

"Ya, the broads are waitin' to give the winner a great big victory kiss." Ned Green purses his thick lips obscenely.

"Matter of fact, Paula is givin' a little spread out at the house," Joey says.

"What's the matter with you, Joey, you're pure as the driven snow," says Ned Green.

"Not pure, you mean driven as the driven snow," says J.B. Then, turning to Joey, he smiles: "As Cardinal Newman might have said, 'The night is dark and I am far from home, lead thou me on, Joey Hopper!'"

Joey turns to Beverly Lambert, who has dressed for this proletarian triumph in a new Dior ensemble. "What's he talkin' about, toots?"

Beverly says crisply, "He's talking about himself. He might have been one of the greats in the labor movement. Now it's all gone to Cadillacs and chateaubriands—and, oh yes, the summer camps for workers' children. Let's never forget the summer camps."

19

In Joey Hopper's unpretentious $25,000 house in a working-class district of the city, Paula is trying to be a hostess. There are drinks and sandwiches on the dining-room table, and Paula fusses around her guests: J. B. Archer, Ned Green, Ace Huddicker, and other union functionaries, including the amused Beverly Lambert. Of the men, only Archer is stylish and really charming. The others are gross, self-satisfied ex-hardhats with big shoulders, expanding bellies, and bright, flowered ties. Uncomfortable with respectable women, they strain to make polite conversation with Paula.

How do you like the city, ma'am? Well, pretty much,

Paula flutters. Frankly, she liked it better when they were still living in the Broadmore. She doesn't know any people in the neighborhood and, of course, Joey is out almost every night working, organizing, attending meetings. . . .

Yeah, this Joey sure is a pistol, they agree. A regular dynamo. Since he came into the area they've picked up forty thousand new members, more than twenty thousand from his spectacular gas-station campaign alone. That's a million in dues right there, Ned Green points out. Mrs. Hopper must be awful proud of him.

Oh she is, she is, she assures them. Though she has to admit—sometimes she does get a little homesick for Hendersonville.

A Siamese cat runs in, chased by another. She swoops them up and hugs them to her. "If it wasn't for Duke 'n' Duchess, and all the movies you can see here that you can't back home, I think I'd go out of my mind."

"Yes, ma'am, they is sure two beautiful kitties," Ace Huddicker purrs.

A small bedroom in the back of the house has been set up as a makeshift gymnasium, with barbells, dumbbells, and a punching bag. Joey has led J.B. here to get away from the others. J.B. takes a playful poke at the bag and it slips off his knuckles.

"Like *this*," Joey says, and taps the bag into rhythmic motion almost like a professional boxer.

"Well, where do we go from here, Muscles?" J.B. says lightly.

"Now we go after all the gas stations in the three surrounding states," Joey says, still hitting the bag.

"You do that every day?" J.B. asks.

"Every morning six on the nose."

J.B. shakes his head. "And one of the things I enjoy about being a labor leader is sleeping late in the morning. Punching in at dawn is for the drivers, not that I don't feel for the drivers."

Joey finishes his flurry with a tremendous hook that almost tears the bag from its socket. "I figure everything that has to do with wheels—even remotely—belongs to us. The gas stations, the car washers, the garage monkeys, even the car-dealer salesmen in their tight white collars."

"We aren't doing too badly the way we are," J.B. says. "A million members."

"My way will double it in five years," Joey says.

"Well, we can take up the expansion and request for new charters at the next Tri-State Conference."

"Oh, that reminds me, J.B.," Joey says, slipping his arm around Archer, "some of the boys think maybe I ought to be chairman of the Tri-State."

"But it's already got a chairman, Joey. His name is J. B. Archer."

"With my gas-station locals, and the Hendersonville Joint Council, and the pull I've got with the brewery boys and the cabdrivers, I've got the votes to beat you, J.B."

Archer is flabbergasted. Ever since he brought him in from the sticks he has been proud of Joey Hopper as his discovery, his protégé. But even caught by surprise he doesn't lose the charm and savoir-faire of the Late Show idol he resembles.

"After all, Joey, I'm a vice-president of the International. It would hardly look proper for a vice-president to serve under a local officer on the Tri-State."

"Oh yeah," Joey goes on, "now that the old crook up in Chicago kicked the bucket—what's his name, Donnelly?—there's a vacancy on the V-P roster. According to the constitution, the president can appoint a substitute until the next convention. I want you to get Bill Reed to give me that slot."

Archer looks at Joey in amazement, in defeat, in admiration. "Yes, sir, Mr. Vice-President," he says with mock, but at the same time, genuine deference. "Will there be anything else?"

Joey slams J.B. on the back, hard. "Let's go back and grub down some o' Paula's lousy ham sandwiches before she starts feelin' even more sorry for herself!"

They go back to the dining room, arm in arm.

In the Senate Committee Hearing Room, now it's Allie Stotzer who is in the question box. Stotzer is foppishly dressed, with a checkered vest and bow tie, halfway between J. Press and show biz, flamboyant, with a carefully combed flare of dark, curly hair. He is intellectually vain, a psychological five inches short of six feet. Educated at the University of Chicago, but drawn early to Chicago's invisible empire, he finds it easy to talk about ideals, ideas, American principles. Allie Stotzer has what amounts to a genius for misappropriating the slogans of democracy to camouflage the underworld-upperworld axis that is working to control it.

The chairman, Senator McAllen, is asking: "Now, Mr. Stotzer, when you classify yourself as a labor-management consultant, am I to understand that your firm, Alvin Stotzer Associates, serves both labor and management with impartiality?"

Stotzer speaks rapidly, with aggressive confidence. "In a sense you might call that our mission, Mr. Chairman. After all, labor and management are partners in what I consider the greatest business in the world—the United States of America. My firm is set up to interpret labor to capital, capital to labor, minimizing disputes and easing areas of friction."

Dennis Crawford asks, "Mr. Stotzer, while you are serving this noble mission, isn't it true that Stotzer Associates has grossed more than eight and a half million dollars in the past five years?"

Stotzer: "That may be. I consider myself the creative head of Stotzer Associates. You would have to ask my chief accountant."

"We would be delighted to question your chief accountant, Mr. Stotzer," Crawford says, "but Mr. Santoro tells me he's had considerable difficulty in locating him."

Allie Stotzer counters, "I don't think this august body would blame a man for having infectious hepatitis."

"Yes, so his doctor advised us," Crawford says.

Drawls a Senator from South Carolina, hoping the

line of investigation stays as far from his state as possible,
"Mr. Crawford, what is the general line of questioning
you wish to direct at Mr. Stotzer's accountant?"

"According to the checks studied by investigator
Santoro," Crawford answers, consulting his notes, "in two
and a half years Mr. Stotzer paid out over two hundred
thousand dollars in behalf of the president of the IBHT,
Mr. Bill Reed. It includes an interesting variety of items,
from television sets to yachts, from nylons to baby's dia-
pers. But we would like to postpone that questioning
until Mr. Reed is called—which may be in the near fu-
ture. Meantime, sir, with your permission, I would like to
question Mr. Stotzer about his subsequent association
with Mr. Joey Hopper."

Allie Stotzer, self-assured, lights a cigarette with a
gold lighter. "Let's take one question at a time, Mr.
Crawford. You and I had several discussions about Mr.
Reed's finances."

Crawford follows him: "All right, if you want to go
back to that, when you or your firm paid out more than
two hundred thousand dollars for Mr. Reed's personal
bills, were you reimbursed by Mr. Reed's personal ac-
count or by the union treasury?"

"As you remember, Mr. Crawford, I suggested that
you meet Mr. Reed face to face in my home to discuss
that matter."

"In a last-minute effort to save his neck."

Stotzer adjusts his tie and smiles. "You have a tend-
ency to put things melodramatically, Mr. Crawford. After

all, Mr. Reed has been an important public figure, a member of the Board of Regents of the State University, a dollar-a-year adviser to the Defense Department, decorated by the President for his patriotic services, a prominent member of four different fraternal orders, national cochairman of the Community Charity drive, a respected churchman, twice chosen Man of the Year for his state . . ."

"We have his record as a public figure, Mr. Stotzer. That may save us some time. Seventeen lines in Who's Who."

"Thank you," Allie Stotzer says, "I thought it was for the good of the country that we work out some understanding that would safeguard the reputation of a man of such national achievement as Mr. F. William Reed."

Crawford exchanges quick looks with his investigating team. He is impatient with all this fancy verbal footwork. It makes him more blunt than usual.

"Isn't it true that when you invited me to your home in the hope of working out some deal with Mr. Reed—and found we weren't buying—that you made a spot decision to desert the sinking ship called 'Honest Bill' Reed and to throw your weight to a likely successor? And wasn't your candidate Mr. Joey Hopper?"

Allie Stotzer runs a quick hand over his curly black hair. "Isn't that rather invidious, Mr. Crawford? As a labor-relations consultant dedicated to furthering the interests of my client, in this case the IBHT, naturally I would want to help young blood, deserving young

*leaders, reach the top. I'm not denying that Joey Hopper
was at my party. After all, you met him there yourself.
He had caught my eye from the time he took over from
J. B. Archer as head of the Tri-State Conference. . . ."*

20

$\mathcal{T}$he black-tie gathering at Allie Stotzer's home is in the
Washington tradition of how-to-make-acquaintances-and-
lean-on-people. If George Washington didn't sleep in
this house, he should have: It is a lavish establishment,
full of graces the Allie Stotzers have been able to buy, if
not inherit.

Present is an impressive assembly of the upper crust,
for this is Stotzer's business, to cultivate senators and
congressmen, and judges, lobbyists, opinion-makers. Complete with cummerbund and a maroon dress tie, Stotzer
darts about like an attentive poodle, with just the right,
bright remark for this one, a whispered hint to that one—
the fixer at work in a split-level house on a six-figure level.
His wife—once his secretary—is an ideal partner for him:
attractive, southern-smart, ambitious, known as one of
"the ten best hostesses in Washington."

Honest Bill Reed is here, a big self-important, overstuffed personage, surrounded by his lackeys. Governor Thayne Winslow is here, although he is an ex-Governor now, having lost the election as he feared following that eventful strike of Petroleum Drivers Local 101. Allie Stotzer commiserates with him. Winslow shrugs it off theatrically. That's politics. Fortunately, he has his health, a lucrative law practice, and a host of friends. Stotzer, operating every moment, suggests that he might be able to do business with the IBHT. With all this investigating going on, perhaps the Governor could use his influence among his party associates on the Senate Committee.

The election may be over but the Thayne Winslow record plays on: "Like you, Mr. Stotzer, I'm for harmony between capital and labor. Whenever I can do my bit to eliminate strife and dissension, you will find me ready to make my contribution."

"Glad you feel that way, Governor," Stotzer says, handing him a highball from the butler's tray. "These are critical times for the IBHT. I think you could be of service."

The ex-Governor mumbles his practiced, bromidic gratitude and Stotzer moves on to greet George Henderson III. George is with his wife, Ashley, a brittle, highbred blonde he doesn't see too often. She skis at St.-Moritz and skin dives in the Bahamas and spends as little time with George as possible. This doesn't disturb him.

Stotzer congratulates George on the remarkable expansion of Henderson & Son. From an upstate dynasty, they have become a tri-state dynasty and are rapidly on the way to achieving national importance. Allie says he himself was lucky to get in early, when the stock went on the Big Board shortly after the gas-station strike that crippled most of Henderson's competitors. "How do you do it, George?"

"I owe it all to Nietzsche—and Joey Hopper, two of my favorite philosophers," George laughs, reaching for another scotch from the butler, and at the same time nodding toward Joey and Paula at the other side of the room. Although this is their debut in Washington high society, Joey refuses to wear a tuxedo. The farthest he'll go is a dark suit. Paula wears a new evening gown, but it isn't enough to give her the confidence she would like to have. She has never been with such high-level people before. She confesses to Joey as she takes a martini from the butler's tray that she feels out of place and doesn't know exactly what to say.

"Tough," Joey says. "You're Mrs. Joey Hopper. Just remember that—that's all you have to say. They'll do the rest. They better!"

Paula looks across at Beverly Lambert, completely at home anywhere, with Lou Vass, Thayne Winslow's assistant, as her escort tonight because Mrs. Archer is present. Paula could be one of the most attractive women here if she felt more protected. "Joey, do you love me?" she asks, out of context.

"Didn't I tell you once?" Joey is annoyed at the distraction.

"Yes, but that was like—a hundred years ago," Paula says.

"Well, when I change my mind, I'll let ya know." Joey is already looking past her. A simple woman who needs simple answers, Paula wishes she were back in Muscle Hollow. She wishes she were Edna.

A blank-faced butler approaches. "Drink, Madame?"

"Yeah, a gibson—a double," Paula says.

"Easy," Joey says. "Easy, Paula. This is big people."

Paula looks at him, so sober, so assured, so many barbells at six o'clock in the morning, so many local-cartage gimmicks. "Make it a triple gibson," she tells the butler.

"Yes, Madame." He bows and turns away.

"Yes, *Madame*," Paula mimics him, just a little tipsy.

"Louse me up here and I'll break your arm," Joey says in an undertone.

"I love you, Joey," Paula says in the same private voice, "I won't louse you up, I just—wish I wasn't here." She brushes at her eyes, knowing she mustn't cry.

Relaxing in a book-lined den are J. B. Archer and a few other vice-presidents of the International. Allie Stotzer enters self-importantly: "Dennis Crawford just came in with his wife. I'm putting him in the rumpus room with Bill Reed. *Vamos a ver*, as we used to say in Havana."

In the rumpus room, Bill Reed in his bulging tuxedo, with small eyes like BBs in his overfed face, studies his man. Dennis Crawford looks like a worried college senior in the age when the music turned from hot to cool.

"I'm delighted we finally had a chance to meet personally," Bill Reed opens. He always sounds as if he were speaking from a podium. "I've long been opposed to

racketeering in my union. I think it is reprehensible—as
dangerous as communism. I welcome any help in clean-
ing it up."

Allie Stotzer beams and pours the Chivas. "You see, I
knew if you two boys met face to face, there wouldn't be
any problem."

"Mr. Reed, as a cobeliever in honest trade unionism,
I'm delighted to have your offer of cooperation," Crawford ploys, nursing, not really drinking, his highball.
"Now—as I am sure you understand—we will naturally
have to ask you certain questions based on information
our staff has been gathering. Somewhat damaging information, as you can well imagine."

Stotzer breaks in. "But Denny, if Bill offers to cooperate, say off the record or in executive session that
wouldn't be released to the press . . ."

Crawford sets his drink down. "Al, if you asked me
here to make a deal with Mr. Reed, I'm sorry you invited
me. I came to appeal to him as the General President of
the largest union in America—and not just the largest, but
the key to transportation, food, the movement of vital
materials—I came to ask him: Can he, in good conscience
as a union man, as one of the key figures in American life
—*will* he come into our Committee and take the Fifth? In
other words, will he say that the questions we ask, on the
basis of months and months of careful investigation, will
tend to incriminate him?"

Bill Reed flushes. He is a very important man. He is
accustomed to having problems like this smoothed out for
him by a running interference of fixers and loophole lawyers. "I thought this was going to be a friendly talk."

"So did I," Crawford says evenly.

"If I had suspected this was going to be an investigation, I would have asked my lawyer, Governor Winslow, to be present."

Crawford rises. "Mr. Stotzer is a lawyer, among other things. And anyway, this is not an investigation, Mr. Reed. Of course, you can bring Stotzer, Winslow, or anyone else you choose to serve as counsel when you are summoned." He turns to his disappointed host. "Thanks again for asking me, Al, but if you thought he could charm me out of this—then I'd say his charm, like his luck, may be running out." He extends his hand to the pale and shaken General President. "See you again, Mr. Reed."

In contrast to Bill Reed's shock, Allie Stotzer is strangely poised, as if nothing had happened. "Jan must be wondering if I kidnapped you. Come on back to the party and I'll find her for you."

"Thanks, but then we'll have to go," Crawford says. "I'm not in a party mood. I still have a lot of work to do tonight."

"Be seeing you, Denny," Bill Reed says with the voice of a wounded buffalo.

"In the Hearing Room," Crawford says as he exits.

Allie Stotzer darts back into the den where J. B. Archer and other International officers are waiting and drinking. "It's no sale," Allie reports. It's exactly what he had feared. Crawford won't play ball. He wants Honest Bill to answer his questions—in open session.

Thayne Winslow, who combines the Tip O'Neill look

with some of Ed Bennett Williams' shrewdness, shakes his head. "In all good conscience, I cannot allow President Reed to answer those questions. Bill has a responsibility to the union, but he also has a responsibility to himself."

Allie Stotzer cuts him off. "Okay, Gov, I get the message. But if we—or rather if Honest Bill throws himself to the wolves, who's going to lead the IBHT? It could be chaos."

This is what J. B. Archer has been waiting for. "Allie, that's why I asked you to invite Joey Hopper down to Washington. He's our ace in the sleeve."

A number of vice-presidents protest. After all, Joey Hopper is only a ninth vice-president. They outrank him. In his own area he's come along very fast, but nationally he's practically a nobody.

"Exactly," Archer counters, "and that's his main strength. If Bill Reed goes down, so does the second vice-president, and the third and the fourth—all of you! Down the toilet! But Joey Hopper can run at the next convention as an outsider, a reformer, a maverick, a rank-and-filer. A new broom for the clean sweep that the members and the public will be looking for."

The smoke-filled den is affected by J.B.'s eloquence. Okay, bring 'im in.

In the spacious living room, where Joey is pointedly not drinking, just watching and taking everything in, Mrs. Stotzer tells him Allie would like to see him. Beverly Lambert, careful to keep mild Lou Vass at her side to allay Mrs. Archer's suspicions, tells Paula that things are *happening.* Paula doesn't understand. Beverly is acid-sweet. "You don't have to understand. Just be your own dear rank-and-file, gibson-guzzling self."

"I sure wish people would talk so I could understand 'em," Paula says wistfully.

Mrs. Stotzer ushers Joey Hopper into the den. If he is a little out of his element, he is still wary and street-smart enough to know how to handle himself. He senses something is up, something big. He hasn't failed to notice that International President Reed returned to the party less sure of himself than when he left it. He senses the significance of Dennis Crawford's hurried exit. He knows that he is being judged by the kingmakers. Well, time to turn the tables: *He* will judge them.

Allie Stotzer opens with the admission that Bill Reed has been subpoenaed and will soon be called as a witness before the McAllen Committee.

Relaxed in an armchair, Joey mutters a noncommittal uh-huh. He has a way of putting his so-called superiors off-balance, forcing them to come up with answers that tip the scales against them, leaving them subservient. Even the fast-talking Stotzer finds himself hesitating. "So—so if Bill should fail to survive the investigation, the leaders of the IB will naturally be looking for a new president."

Joey Hopper doesn't give them an inch. "So?"

After an awkward pause, J. B. Archer speaks up. "Joey, I might as well level. I suggested to these gentlemen that if anything should happen to Bill, I think you would make a brilliant president." He turns to the cluster of VP's. "Right, boys?"

When Joey stands up, he dominates the room. "Gentlemen, I'm flattered. J.B., believe me, I appreciate the personal support. But I am an organization man. At the moment I have the honor to be the Ninth Vice-President. My obligation is to support our International President until he is proven guilty or chooses to resign his high office. Thank you, gentlemen."

He makes his exit. He knows he has them. Exactly where he wants them. Hanging.

"What do you think?" J.B. asks.

Although he holds no office in the union, Stotzer is the first to speak.

"I think you found yourself a genius."

The mealy-mouthed vice-presidents, growing fat on their forty to fifty thousand a year, their Cadillacs, their expense accounts, and the soft touches that elevate many to the hundred-thousand-a-year bracket, mutter their agreement.

Allie hurries out to escort Crawford and Jan to their car. "Thanks for dropping in, Denny, it was an honor."

"I have to give you an A for effort, Al." Stotzer thinks he's opaque, but to Crawford he's a picture window. "I'm not playing games."

"Look, I admire you," Stotzer says, and then adds almost casually, "Oh, by the way, if you want to pick up a few interesting facts about Bill's new country estate, Idlewood Farms, you might talk to the contractor, Frank

Williamson. Well, good night, Denny. My pleasure, Mrs. Crawford."

As they drive off, Jan asks, "He's a crawly little man. Is he really trying to help you against his own client?"

"Who knows? I think it's worth my flying out and seeing this Mr. Williamson myself. The way Stotzer plays it, if he's betting the favorite and it breaks down, he's got another winner moving up on the inside."

In the crowded, hectic living room, Bill Reed is waiting anxiously for Allie. "He's a tough kid," Bill says. "This isn't gonna be like that investigation we breezed through two years ago."

"Don't worry, Bill." Stotzer has to reach up to pat him on the shoulder. "Governor Winslow and I are still in your corner."

"I wish I had followed my hunch and left for Europe before that subpoena."

"Don't forget the Governor still has a couple of friends on that Committee," Allie tries to cheer him up.

"But that kid," Bill Reed continues to fret. "He's got a mean look in his eye."

"*Mean* we could handle. Trouble is, I'm afraid he's honest. Difficult type to deal with." Allie Stotzer hurries off to play host to Joey Hopper and his pretty fish-out-of-water, Paula.

"Come on over. I want you to meet Judge Fulton," Allie says, steering them toward an important-looking guest. Stotzer winks at Joey familiarly, already beginning to take him under his wing. "A friend at court never did anybody any harm, right, Joe?"

"I'm with ya," Joey says, and, in a hoarse aside to Paula, "No more fa you, honey. This ain't no party. We're here for blood."

The next witness before the Senate Committee is International General President F. William Reed. This is one of the major events of the hearing and the room is jammed with spectators, reporters, press photographers, and television cameras. Also present, strategically separated and watchfully awaiting developments, are Allie Stotzer, J. B. Archer, and Joey Hopper.

Crawford has begun the questioning: "Mr. Reed, we are ready to enter as exhibits eleven checks amounting to $225,203.19 for such personal items as a fifty-four-foot yacht, two television sets, three dozen monogrammed silk shirts, and a number of other purchases that our investigator Mr. Santoro is prepared to itemize. Do you deny that these items, paid for from the union treasury, were for your personal use and enjoyment?"

Bill Reed is like a giant balloon shrinking from a helium leak. "I respectfully decline to answer. Under the Fifth Amendment to the Constitution . . ."

There is excited murmuring in the Hearing Room and a barrage of photo flashes. Chairman McAllen pounds for order. Then he says, "Mr. Reed, you are the president of the largest and most powerful union in America. You are no ordinary labor goon with a prison record. Does a man of your tremendous responsibility and influence really want to tell this Committee and your country, 'I refuse to say whether or not I misused union funds because the answer will tend to incriminate me'? Is that what you want to tell your own members and your fellow-citizens?"

Bill Reed flushes. "Mr. Chairman, my counsel is Governor Thayne Winslow, known to you as a distinguished and honored public servant. It is on his advice that I exercise my privilege under the Constitution of these great United States."

Crawford turns to the chairman. "Would you ask Mr. Reed to stand aside temporarily while we call Mr. Frank Williamson?"

A fat-on-muscle middle-aged man with thinning red hair, Frank Williamson takes the stand. His construction company was paid $280,000, he testifies, to remodel Idlewood Farms, Mr. Reed's estate. This included, among other items, a tennis court, extensive landscaping, a sixty-foot swimming pool, the stocking of a private trout pond, and a stable for a dozen trotting horses.

"And when you submitted your bill, by whom was it paid, Mr. Williamson?"

"It was paid by the union," Williamson answers.

Crawford nods. "Mr. Chairman, we would like to introduce as Exhibit 147 the check number 9722 bearing the signature of the treasurer of the IBHT against the union account with the Washington Trust & Savings Bank of this city."

The chairman says, "Thank you, Mr. Williamson, for your forthright testimony. It is refreshing to have some people come here and tell the simple truth. You may be excused. Now, will Mr. Reed come around?"

"Honest Bill" Reed, intimate of Governors and even Presidents, who has been called a "great labor statesman" and a "giant among men," has the eyes of a bull no longer strong enough to charge, waiting for the matador to come to him.

"Mr. Reed, with the $225,000 expended for you by Stotzer Associates and the $280,000 paid by the union for your own private estate, you have taken—and we consider this a minimum figure—some $505,000 from the International Brotherhood you supposedly serve. Do you feel that if you gave a truthful answer to whether or not you stole some $505,000 of union funds, that it would tend to incriminate you?"

President Reed opens his mouth as if he needs more air to breathe. "It might," he mumbles.

Crawford is exasperated. "Mr. Reed, 'might' is an evasive answer. I should think a man in your high position would want to tell his million members directly: Did you, or did you not, steal approximately half a million dollars from those members?"

Reed gulps. "On the advice of my counsel, the Honorable Governor Thayne Winslow . . ."

"Since you seem so fond of invoking the name of the Honorable Governor Thayne Winslow," Crawford breaks in, "I think the record should show, with no disrespect for Mr. Winslow, that he is now ex-Governor Winslow."

The questioning continues, and Bill Reed, who has loved the image of himself as a patriotic public figure, is reduced to muttering, "I must decline on the grounds that my answer may tend to incriminate me."

*As Reed pronounces his own death sentence as head
of the IBHT, Allie Stotzer, J. B. Archer, and his Girl
Friday-through-Sunday look across the room to study
Joey Hopper's reaction. Joey wears his poker-face. But his
mind is working like an IRS computer.*

21

*F*rom Bill Reed's Senate Committee debacle, Joey Hopper returns to his small house in Capital City with J. B.
Archer and Beverly Lambert. Lu, the black maid—at last
the Hoppers do have a part-time maid—tells them Mrs.
Hopper is out looking at the new house they have been
thinking of buying. J.B. and Beverly drive out there with
Joey—it is in the affluent suburb of Capital City called
Sherwood Hills. They find Paula in the newly built
mansion, with her sister, Edna, whom Paula has invited
down from Hendersonville both to ease her loneliness
and to show her the house.

"I hear ya gettin' married to Art," Joey says to Edna.
"Nice goin', you two kids deserve each other."

If it is a double-edged compliment, Paula is too excited to notice it. The new house has her enthralled: the grounds, the huge master bedroom with a sunbathing porch, her own dressing room, a billiard room, and the kitchen and pantry, which seem as large as the entire little stucco house they have been living in. The real-estate lady feels sure of a sale. "I knew you'd love it. And it's really a steal at ninety-five thousand with a sixty-thousand mortgage on easy terms."

"It's a showplace, all right," J.B. agrees. "If you're short of cash, you can borrow sixty thou from the Tri-State Conference."

"I don't want it," Joey says flatly.

Paula is shocked. And even more so when Joey adds, "I just made up our mind. We're gonna stay where we are."

"In that lousy little barn? Why, it isn't even as big as Art and Edna's—and after all, you are a vice-president."

"Right. And when the next convention is over, maybe even higher than that."

J.B. looks at him, pleased. "You've decided to run?"

Joey says, "You're lookin' at the goddamnedest rank-and-file reform candidate your union ever seen. Reform candidates don't live in no palaces for ninety-five thousand clams." He looks around at its grandeur. "I think you ought to take it, J.B. It fits your personality. You like to live it up. And it'll be a nice meetin' place for those big shots of labor, industry, and all the rest of the high polloi you're so good at butterin' up. I'll see that the Conference loans you the down payment."

Paula runs out to the car in tears. Edna follows to console her sister. In an undertone, Beverly tells Joey,

"I'm glad I'm not married to you, killer. But if you want to dictate some letters in my apartment some night . . ."

"If I c'n find the time." Joey gives nothing. "I'm gonna be awful busy."

22

————◆————

*H*ome again, Joey is energetically emptying his dresser drawers and closets of all his fancy clothes. No more silk monogrammed shirts. No more faggy Italian suits that J.B. touted him onto. No more fifty-dollar shoes. Deliberately he puts on his old pair from Hendersonville.

"But I was just gonna give those to the Salvation Army," Paula protests. "Look at the holes in the soles."

"That's the way I'm gonna wear 'em."

"But why, why—you're making forty thousand a year —and J.B. says . . ."

"Let J.B. have the silk shirts and the big house in Sherwood Hills and Beverly Lambert. J.B. c'n make beautiful speeches about social justice for the workin' man, but he's gone about as far as he can go."

At the same time that he is dressing down, looking more like the Joey Hopper who first arrived in Capital City, he brings out some papers he wants Paula to sign.

"What are they, Joey?"

"Don't ask questions, just sign 'em," he orders. They seem to make her president of the P. S. Company.

"What is the P. S. Company? I don't understand."

"You don't have to understand. Just sign where Mr. Nettles put the X's."

"Nettles? Isn't he George Henderson's chief account-ant?"

"Sign it, goddamn it, sign it! Don't ask so many fuckin' questions!"

Paula signs obediently, or rather, fearfully, and pours herself a glass of ale.

"Paula, you gotta cut out this drinkin'," Joey says. "Look at ya. Ya useta have the best shape in Muscle Hol-low."

"I know," she says, and nods toward a sexy picture of herself in her cheerleader costume, the way she looked when she was rooting for Joey in the Hendersonville bowling alleys. "But you're away so much, Joey, it sorta keeps my mind off things, this an' Duke 'n' Duchess." She strokes one of the Siamese cats purring in her lap.

"Look at me," Joey says, pounding his stomach with his fist. "I haven't gained two pounds since I climbed off the trucks."

"I know," Paula says, "that's you, Joey, flat and hard."

"Tough," he says. "You know you're stuck with me."

"Joey." Begging. "All I ask is be nice. Just every once in a while be nice. Like right now, why don't you take me to the Lobster House and then to the movie? It's that beautiful Richard Burton. He plays the stepfather of Jane Fonda, only when his wife dies in childbirth . . ."

"Look, Paula, I got no time for that crap. I'm runnin' for president of the IBHT. I gotta be all over the country these next four weeks. I'm gonna make Honest Bill Reed fold up like a broken accordion. He's a big nothin'. Soft and dumb."

"I know," Paula says wretchedly. "And you—you're hard—and flat—and smart."

Joey pauses a moment. For a second or two he feels sorry for Paula: once the belle of Muscle Hollow, now beginning to flounder in ale and Siamese cats and loneliness. "Okay, tell you what I'll do with ya," he says. "Get dolled up an' I'll take ya t' the Kit Kat Klub."

"The Kit Kat," Paula says. "Isn't that the joint where there was a murder a couple of months ago? The police arrested the owner, One Eye Cicero?"

"Honey, Vinnie Cicero was out in twenty-four hours. The cops didn't have a thing on 'im. I've met 'im a couple times and he seems like a pretty nice fella."

Called to the witness chair before the Senate Committee is Vincent ("One Eye") Cicero. He's handsome, dark-haired, dark-eyed, dressed in a dark silk suit with a white silk tie and a squared white silk handkerchief. His good looks are marred only by the black patch he wears over one eye, though it is as carefully tailored as the Hathaway-shirt man's. Even with these accoutrements, he is not the tough-talking Hollywood stereotype of the gangster. He is soft-spoken, even rather well-spoken, with only occasional grammatical lapses; doing his best to pass for a gentleman. Flanked by his lawyers, Cicero is also attended by some of his boys: the elephantine Tiny Lake, Three Fingers Jones, and other loyal acolytes of the Black Mass.

Vincent Cicero identifies himself as a labor leader. He represents locals of bartenders, restaurant workers, racetrack employees, and music-machine technicians.

"By music machines, I presume you mean jukeboxes?" Dennis Crawford asks.

"We call them music-vending machines. If you want to call them jukeboxes, there is no law against jukeboxes."

"Now, these locals of yours—our display will show twenty-one different charters in all—were expelled from the AFL-CIO as gangster-ridden and unable to meet the code of that organization. Is that not true, Mr. Cicero?"

"The locals under my leadership severed their connection with the AFL-CIO."

"And, shortly before the IBHT convention of last November, they were admitted to the IBHT?"

"I'm proud of my association with the greatest labor organization in the country." With his one good eye, Cicero tries to stare Crawford down.

"And it was shortly after you received the charters from the IB that you swung your support to Mr. Hopper, Mr. Cicero?"

"I thought he was the best man for the job. Anything wrong in that?"

"That is exactly what we are here to find out." Crawford turns to Senator McAllen. "Mr. Chairman, at this time I would like to call Mr. Edelman as a witness."

"*You will step aside but remain present to be recalled,*" *Senator McAllen instructs Vincent Cicero.*

Dave Edelman testifies that over the past several months he has made an investigation into the criminal record and general background of Vincent Cicero. In the 1950s, Cicero spent five years in Sing Sing for second-degree murder. He did another two years in Leavenworth for income-tax evasion. He has a record of seventeen arrests, including two for suspicion of murder and one for alleged trafficking in narcotics. The FBI considers him a member of the Mafia and he has been closely related to Benny Champagne, Big John Moody, Greasy Tie Tugiello, Honeyboy Bassetti, and many other underworld figures. He was present at the seminal Apalachin conference in September 1957. According to police files, he uses labor organizations as a front for extortion and other criminal activities.

Senator McAllen breaks in. "*Let me get this straight. Mr. Cicero has just testified that he backed Mr. Hopper for president of the IBHT because he thought he was the best man for the job. And Mr. Hopper was running on a platform of rank-and-file honesty and trade-union reform to clean up the mess left behind by Mr. 'Honest Bill' Reed. Is that correct?*"

"*As far as I am able to follow it, that is absolutely correct, sir,*" *Dave Edelman answers.*

"*That's what I thought I heard,*" *the chairman says.* "*This thing is like a set of Chinese boxes, you open up one only to discover another. Mr. Chief Counsel, you may proceed. Mr. Cicero is still under oath.*"

"*Mr. Cicero,*" *Crawford picks up the thread,* "*when*

you decided to throw your support—your locals, your influence in Chicago, New York, New Orleans, St. Louis— to Mr. Hopper, there were no under-the-table deals, no fix between you and the union and the 'Democratic Reform' candidate?"

Cicero has to consult with his lawyer. *"Not to the best of my recollection, insofar as I can recall . . ."*

*B*ehind Vincent Cicero's best recollection lies a vivid memory of his meeting with Joey Hopper at the Kit Kat Klub. Cicero is dressed in a white speckled Italian suit, the most elegant in mobdom finery. He even wears a white eyepiece to complement his ensemble. With him is his wife, Monique, a tall redheaded showgirl in sequins and mink stole, with a nasal accent and a good-natured disposition. The floor show is on—frenetic ponies in see-through bras and postage-stamp bikinis—but neither Cicero nor Joey pays much attention. Nearby hovers Tiny Lake, the Kit Kat bouncer and an official of the Bar and Cafe Employees Union, sided by his union associate, Three Fingers Jones, so named because two digits were sacrificed in a long-ago jurisdictional dispute.

Cicero suggests to Monique that she take Paula to the ladies' room so the girls can powder their noses. Unlike Joey, he stands up when they rise to leave. As soon as he has Joey alone—despite the blaring of the band accompanying the pony chorus, who are doing an oriental number to satisfy the current oriental fad, with the emcee crooning "I Was Happy-Happy-Happy with My Jappy-Jappy-Japanese Gal"—Cicero turns his back on the exotic bumps and grinds to get down to cases. The word is going around that Joey Hopper has a better than even chance to knock out the incumbent, Bill Reed, for the presidency of the IBHT. To make it virtually a sure thing, Joey could have Cicero's now-independent locals taken into the IBHT. That would give him at least sixty additional delegates. On top of that, Cicero's boys, enforcers like Tiny Lake and Three Fingers, could be electioneering for Joey. They are extremely persuasive vote-getters, Cicero says.

"What's the price?" Joey cuts through.

"Just a simple favor," says Vincent Cicero. "I'm worried about my eldest kid, Vincent, Junior. I love the kid like nothin' human on earth. Me, I had to fight my way up in small fight clubs—I got exactly three hundred dollars for losing this eye—the bum fought me with his thumb in my eyeball for eight rounds. So I want for Junior to go into the insurance business—like you give 'im just the Tri-State account alone, I figure he could cut fifteen percent commission on a hundred million bucks in three or four years. This health-and-welfare thing is rubies 'n' diamonds an' every once in a while Junior can hand you a little brown envelope."

"Vince, if I can swing the Tri-State insurance to your kid, why not? But I ain't in the labor movement to get rich."

"Sure, Joey, I know, you're the reform candidate. But you know what I always say, 'Green vegetables is good for the digestion.'"

The Happy-Jappy production number mercifully has come to an end. The wives return. Paula is in high spirits. This is the most fun she's had since she came to Capital City. Monique Cicero is just as sweet as she can be.

"Me and your old man are hitting it off pretty good, too," Vince says. "Maybe the four of us can go steady."

The emcee-comic puts the spotlight on Joey and Paula—"A young man who has come a long way in a short time, a credit to the labor movement and to the good old U.S. of A., and his charming better half—I may not be an expert on transportation like Joey Hopper, but I know a good chassis when I see one!"

Paula waves in the spotlight, both pleased and embarrassed, a momentary balm for the lonely nights.

In the Senate Committee Hearing Room, the questioning of union fashion plate J. B. Archer is continuing. Archer has consistently tried to portray himself as an honest and idealistic labor leader, doing his best to further in the IBHT the genuine trade-union principles he first learned in the CIO. . . .

"*And that is how I continue to consider myself,*" J.B. *insists.*

"*Then how can you reconcile your professed*

idealism with bringing into the IBHT men of the ilk of Vincent 'One Eye' Cicero?" Crawford asks.

J. B. Archer obviously is not happy with his answer. "We have a constitution ninety-seven pages long. We have our own international machinery for judging the merits and demerits of men of the caliber of Mr. Cicero."

"That isn't quite answering my question, Mr. Archer." Crawford tries to hold him on the hook. "Didn't you have a row with Mr. Joey Hopper about the injection of Vincent Cicero and his mob—we may as well call it by its right name—into the Hopper election campaign?"

"Who told you that?" J.B. asks.

"Our investigators, Mr. Edelman and Mr. Mahoney, spent ten days in Capital City shortly before the Convention. I am sure they will be glad to testify under oath to what they learned from reliable sources—including, incidentally, your wife, Helen Archer."

J.B.'s answer is temperate. "Look, I might have said something to Joey about hoping this would be an honest election. I probably did, since I continue to believe in them."

"So do we, Mr. Archer," Crawford says. "That's one of our chief purposes here, to help those unions that have strayed far and wide from democratic procedure."

"Mr. Crawford, believe me, I respect what you're trying to do," J.B. says with apparent sincerity. "But these things have to be handled from the inside."

"Isn't that what the whale said to Jonah?"

Everyone in the Hearing Room laughs or smiles, except Dennis Crawford and J. B. Archer.

24

———————◆———————

What J.B. would not or could not tell Dennis Crawford, out of loyalty to the union and to Joey, is that they'd
had heated words about the incursion of Vincent Cicero
into the IBHT family. The confrontation had taken place
in J.B.'s splendidly furnished mansion, the one Joey
palmed off on him after seeing what conspicuous con-
sumption had done to the reputation of Honest Bill
Reed.

In these plush surroundings, J. B. Archer, uneasy
mixture of legitimate trade unionist and high-living he-
donist, worries aloud about Joey's new alliance with Vincent Cicero. J.B. considers Cicero one of the most dangerous labor racketeers in the country. Those locals of his are
unions in name only—actually little more than shakedown
outfits with organizers like Tiny Lake and Three Fingers
Jones, whose organizing methods lean toward dynamite
and lead. J.B. is reconciled to the fact that General President Reed is a crook. But Honest Bill is a far different
kind of crook from Vincent Cicero—pretty much a good-
natured slob with luxurious tastes who stole perhaps half
a million from the union treasury and looked the other

way while some of his henchmen also reached into the till. But at least he had no direct ties to the underworld. In J.B.'s morality this is an important difference.

Joey is unmoved. "Sometimes, J.B., you've got to go where the power is. Sure Vinnie One Eye is a 'dinosaur'—isn't that what you call 'em?"

"I call them worse than that," J.B. says.

"But he can open a lot of doors, get me into cities where the mob has us blocked out. With his delegates at the Convention, and the legitimate locals you can bring along, I think I'll have it made. Once we have the power, we can throw the bums out—or at least keep 'em in line."

"That'll be the day," J.B. says. "I think you underestimate a dinosaur."

Joey is becoming impatient with the lecture. "Look, J.B., you work your egghead side of the street like that statement of policy I wanna put in the hotel box of every delegate."

"The Ten Commandments of Union Democracy," J.B. says. "I roughed out a draft this afternoon, Joey."

"Good. Have two thousand copies run off."

"Don't you want to read it first? It's got a good strong plank on racketeers, crooks, communists, and fascists."

"The stronger the better," says Joey.

"And it pulls no punches about unethical financial practices and about extending the rights of individual locals and members."

"Sounds swell. Print it up real pretty."

"But, Joey, how are we going to make good on this platform if we've got the dinosaurs?"

"J.B., you got dinosaurs on the brain," Joey laughs.

"Broads I like," J.B. admits. "Good scotch I like. Cadillacs I like. Imported tweeds I like. A little expense-account juggling I don't mind, as long as we give our members something for their money. But you've got to keep your hoods out of my hair, Joey. I can't stand the smell of them—literally the perfume: I can smell them a block away."

"J.B., stop being an old woman. You handle social advancements, pensions, medical insurance, clinics, and I'll back you all the way. After all, ain't we gettin' more for our men than they ever got before?"

"Yes," the ambivalent, troubled Archer has to admit. "Except in certain soft areas where favored bosses seem to get preferential treatment. Like Henderson & Son. Already some of their employees are beefing because they're taking home twelve-fifty less a week than other gas-station attendants."

"J.B., you polish the policy statement and leave the beefs to me," Joey says.

Helen Archer enters in a night-robe. She is a handsome, intelligent woman of J.B.'s age, but in her husband's eyes, sexually long over the hill. "If you're going to be working late, dear, shall I make some coffee?"

"Don't bother, Mrs. A.," Joey answers for him, "I think we've got everything pretty well nailed for t'night. Right, J.B.?"

Archer nods, then pours himself another Chivas, neat.

Continuing his testimony before the Senate Committee is Art Nielsen. How much did Mr. Nielsen know about the inside manipulations of the campaign for the presidency of the IBHT? Dennis Crawford asks. Art shakes his head. He never had any part of any manipulations.

"All I knew, Mr. Crawford, is what Joey told me the day he came home to see me. Believe me, that was a real big day for Muscle Hollow!"

25

This is Hendersonville revisited. Joey Hopper returning to Muscle Hollow as the small-town boy who made better than good, leading a fleet of black Cadillacs, with Mooney the business agent as his proud chauffeur, followed by J. B. Archer, Beverly Lambert, Ned Green, Ace Huddicker, and other fixtures of IB officialdom.

They drive up to the Nielsen house, the same one Art was living in when Joey left, now modestly improved. Art is a little more settled. After all, he isn't just a tank-truck driver any more, but the head of a thriving Joint Council. Still he is basically unchanged. Edna is at his side, proud to introduce their infant son, Little Joey, named for his famous uncle.

The entranceway is thronged with Joey's old buddies —Porky Porcovich, Deac Johnson, Billy Kasco, and other

charter members of Local 101. Also present is the eight-
een-year-old Tommy Nielsen, whom Joey bangs on the
shoulder—"Sure looks like a chip off the old block."

"Tommy gets his membership card in six months,"
Art says proudly. "He's gonna be a good union man, Joey,
you just watch and see."

"Swell, swell, in this fight we need every good man
we can get," Joey says off the top of his head.

Young Tommy Nielsen doesn't do too much talking.
In his withdrawn way he is watching the Cadillacs, the
union lackeys like Green and Huddicker, the style of Miss
Lambert, the subtle changes in Joey Hopper that Joey
thinks he is hiding under the old-time Muscle Hollow camaraderie: "How's the bowlin' team goin'?—don't tell me
you lost to the Hod Carriers—ya shoulda sent for me—we
woulda murdered them bums!"

Joey knows how to talk their language all right, but
now he is talking it instead of living it. The happy en-
tourage moves on into the house. Paula and Edna manage
to steal a few moments to themselves in the kitchen
while the boys open beer in the front parlor. Edna says
Paula looks wonderful, but they both know the truth—
Paula's expensive clothes and beauty-parlor polish cannot
quite hide her gain in weight or her inner dissatisfaction.

Edna's change has been almost the reverse. She
doesn't look as well as she did—it's a handful to take care
of, with Art, and the baby, and Pinky's widow, Sara, and
her three, and Grandpa Nielsen, who's getting feeble but
still talks militant unionism as strongly as ever. But Edna
manages, and she's happy, even though—she's wanted to
tell her sister this for a long time—she realizes Paula was

the one Art really was in love with and that he took her as second choice. "Maybe if you're real romantic, that means a lot, Paula, but you know, it doesn't make me unhappy. I love Art—he's a good man, he cares about his family, and he's sweet to me—maybe I think I don't ask enough out of life, but that's all the life I need. We're both crazy about Little Joey and Art's doing a fine job with the Council—oh, he'll never get famous like Joey Hopper, but the drivers here in Hendersonville, you should see how much they think of him, Paula, it would do your heart good. . . ."

"Eddie, I'm so happy for you I could cry," Paula says, and seems ready to do just that and vent her own pent-up feelings. "Oh hell, why don't we have a drink together? This is a celebration!"

In the front parlor Joey gets around to what he really came for. He wants Art to nominate him for president at the Convention in Los Angeles. After all, Joey is the rank-and-file reform, anti-fat-cat candidate. What would be more fitting than to have his original rank-and-file buddy, Art Nielsen, put him in nomination against gravy-train-rider Bill Reed?

Art is flattered, flustered. He isn't a public speaker—oh, sure, here in Hendersonville where all the boys know and trust him, he can get up, but at a national convention, with coast-to-coast TV, and a hundred mikes giving him stage fright, he wouldn't know what to say.

"You won't hafta know what to say—J.B. here will write ya the most beautiful speech ya ever gave." Joey pinches Archer's cheek. Even Paula joins in: "You'll have a suite at the Ambassador Hotel, all expenses paid. We've even been invited to spend an afternoon touring the movie studios."

Edna is enchanted with the idea. Art is shy and unsure of himself. But everybody is busy talking him into it. "I even brought you some of my dresses," Paula confides to Edna in an undertone. "They don't fit me any more, but they'll look wonderful on you. The gals really dress up at these conventions. No kiddin', you'd think you were at the State Chamber of Commerce or somethin'. . . ."

The IBHT Convention at the Ambassador Hotel in Los Angeles has all the fanfare, color, and hoopla of a national political convention. Allie Stotzer, who unceremoniously abandoned his old pal Reed after Honest Bill's collapse at the Senate Committee hearings, has put his public-relations machine into high gear. The delegates for Hopper wear loud blazers and snappy straw boaters with Joey's name screaming from the hatband.

Wearing Joey Hopper blazers and led by shapely drum majorettes, a band marches through the lobby with big bass drums emblazoned BEAT THE DRUMS FOR JOEY HOPPER. The majorettes wear tasteless but catchy sashes slanted from bare shoulder to tiny waist: I'M HOT FOR HOPPER.

Meanwhile, Paula, Edna, and other members of the Ladies Auxiliary, wearing oversize Hopper campaign buttons, are passing out copies of J. B. Archer's artful pamphlet, "The Ten Commandments of IBHT Democracy, by Joey Hopper."

Hopper campaign headquarters on the mezzanine are ablaze with flags, placards, and well-wishers, some of them union politicians, but others just plain, honest truck-driver delegates who believe it is time to throw the rascals (Bill Reed and Company) out.

In contrast, Reed's headquarters are rather staid and semideserted. His platform is: Are we going to let the government tell us drivers how to vote? Honest Bill is trying to picture himself as the victim of persecution by antilabor senators.

In the different hotel suites, J. B. Archer is conscientiously working his side of the street, while Vincent Cicero and his fellow dinosaurs work the other. J.B. talks to local delegations about the sound trade-union reforms Jocy Hopper will institute if elected. Cicero tells his boys to buttonhole uncertain delegates and tell them they could wind up face down in the beautiful Pacific if they don't vote for Hopper.

Joey is moving from suite to suite, addressing different local caucuses: New Jersey Local 795, Arkansas Local 73, California Local 505. To each of these gatherings Joey is accompanied by Art Nielsen, Deac Johnson, Porky Porcovich, and other rank-and-file delegates, as well as by tough city men like Ned Green and Ace Huddicker. Wearing blue jeans and a sports shirt, as if he had just climbed off a truck, Joey makes his talks short and pointed: "I'm not wearin' these jeans for a gag. If I lose, I'm ready t' climb back behind the wheel. Hell, it's an easier life than havin' to worry about a million rig-jockeys like you bums."

And then he adds, "No shit, I ain't been away from the pajama wagons so long I forgot what the problems are. Anytime you pass through Capital City, drop in at my joint and have a beer with me. It ain't no three-hundred-thousand-dollar mansion—like some fella I could mention likes t' rattle around in—it's just a nice little twenty-five-thousand-dollar job, probably just about the same as you got, but it's big enough for me and Paula and you c'n take my home phone number and call me night or day if you think I can help ya."

His audience laughs and applauds, he plays them like a yo-yo, while pompous Bill Reed is saying, "As God is my judge, I know that my position before that antilabor Committee was moral and patriotic and I'm proud of my stewardship of this great International organization."

In one of these caucuses, Joey follows the florid incumbent. Joey cracks, "A fella who calls himself 'Honest,' he's a fella you gotta watch out for. It's like my friend, Brother Lake here"—he thumbs toward the three-hundred-pounder grinning at his side—"everybody calls him 'Tiny' for the same reason they call Bill Reed 'Honest.'"

A wave of laughter and big-handed applause sweeps the caucus room.

Art Nielsen's feeling through this whirlwind campaign is one of excitement and confusion, swept along in a strange world he never expected to see. He is wearing a straw hat, Hopper blazer, and a big JOEY FOR JUSTICE button like the rest of the committed delegates.

The enormous grand ballroom of the Ambassador, jammed with thousands of IBHT delegates and friends, reverberates with music, applause, and noise. The podium is banked with flags and flowers and rows of vice-presidents. They face a phalanx of television cameras and radio microphones, while the myriad state delegations overflowing the hall wave their own banners and placards, many of them for Joey Hopper, along with others still for Bill Reed.

Reed has just been nominated for reelection by an old war-horse who started in the beer-wagon days. There is a mechanical demonstration. Now it is Art Nielsen's turn. J. B. Archer and Beverly Lambert are at his side. Art is suffering a bad case of stage fright. Even in his wildest imagination he hadn't pictured a setting as overpowering as this. Edna is with him, squeezing his hand. Paula, with a prominent Hopper sash from shoulder to waist, is helping him, too. Even young Tommy is on hand, quietly wishing his uncle luck and inwardly wondering why they have to put on this much of a show. His dead father's approach to trade unionism was less Madison-Avenued.

Art Nielsen is introduced briefly by J. B. Archer. Art comes haltingly to the microphone. He blinks in the glare of the TV lights. He didn't come here to make a speech, he says. To his surprise this sets off a resounding cheer.

He came to talk about an old rank-and-file buddy of his, he goes on, the guy with whom he and some other stand-up guys, proud to be charter members of Local 101, broke the notorious open-shop system of Henderson County. Joey Hopper was one heck of a picket-line fighter in those days, and Art has come here to this great Convention to nominate him because he and his fellow rank-and-filers are convinced this is exactly what the IBHT needs, not millionaire businessmen masquerading as labor leaders, but militant fighters for workers' rights—"Like the next president of this great International Brotherhood —Brother Joey Hopper!"

The nomination sets off a wild demonstration. Huge blowup pictures of Joey Hopper lead the parade around the hall. The band plays a strident version of "When the Saints Go Marching In." The cute drum majorettes lead the band with the provocative Hopper sashes bouncing against saucy young boobs. Paula is photographed standing on a chair waving a "Joey for Justice" banner. Tiny Lake carries a mammoth circular poster, ten feet high, with a noble drawing of Joey in the center, surrounded by scenes of his labor heroics, with such captions as—*Son of a Labor Martyr Who Died of Silicosis; Drove Everything from Crackle Crates to Petroleum Tankers; Youngest Vice-President in IBHT History; From Picketline Fighter to Tough Negotiator.*

A giant conga line forms behind the band. The chairman pounds his gavel for silence. Various cogs in the Joey Hopper machine, some on the platform, some leading placard-waving delegations, look satisfied: J. B. Archer, Allie Stotzer, Vincent Cicero, "Governor" Thayne Winslow. Beverly Lambert refreshes her lipstick. "How many saints'll be marching in, Jay?" she asks Archer.

Out of the corner of his mouth, he says, "In the immortal words of Ring Lardner, 'Shut up, he explained.'"

It is time for the roll-call vote. The first local president rises to his delegation mike. His diction has a touch of Paul O'Dwyer's just-off-the-boat charm: IBHT Local Number One, organized in the days of horse-drawn wagons, but prepared to recognize a sixteen-cylinder leader when it sees one, casts its sixteen votes for J for justice, T for tough, H for hope and hard work—Joseph T. Hopper!"

There is another ovation and resounding chords of "When the Saints Go Marching In."

With minor variations, other delegations follow suit. There are scattered votes for incumbent Bill Reed, but after the third delegation has been polled, Reed asks to be recognized. His heart has been touched, he says, by the thousands of telegrams he has received from loyal union brothers and by the many delegates he knows are ready to stand by him on the floor of this great Convention. But there comes a time when older men must step aside for new blood—"That is what has made our beloved International Brotherhood the most powerful union in the world." Therefore, in the interest of labor amity, and to save the hardworking delegates weary hours of roll calls, Bill Reed wishes at this time to withdraw. "In favor of the next, great president of the greatest union in the world, Joey Hopper!"

Pandemonium fills the hall. Above the din, reform champion Joey Hopper manages to shout that bygones

are bygones, Brother Reed has given tremendous service
to the International in his twenty years in office, and as
Joey's first act as General President he would like to en-
tertain a motion that Honest Bill Reed be given his home
free-and-clear for life and a pension of fifty thousand dollars a year. This is carried by acclamation. Bill Reed
comes forward and embraces his successor. TV cameras
record the reconciliation. Flashbulbs burst in the air and
the IBHT flag is still there. Bill Reed cries real tears, of
which he always has a ready supply.

Joey Hopper is carried off on the shoulders of his admirers, a strange ensemble running the gamut from Art
Nielsen, Deac Johnson, and other honest Hendersonville
driver-delegates to corruptible pros like Ned Green and
Ace Huddicker—and to Vincent Cicero and his no-non-
sense enforcers, Tiny Lake, Three Fingers, and the rest of
them.

The noisy, colorful Victory Ball in the Ambassador
Hotel's famous Coconut Grove bedazzles Art Nielsen and
Edna—she's been to the beauty parlor and looks almost
glamorous in one of Paula's evening gowns. Art is basking
in some of Joey's reflected glory. There is a good deal of
backslapping and handshaking for his "terrific" nomination speech. The fact that he meant every naïve word of
it, even though some of the most effective words were
shrewdly placed in his stammering mouth by J. B.
Archer, is overlooked. It was a "smart move," he's told. It's
bound to do him a lot of good in the IB now that Joey is
in the driver's seat. Art's protestations that he is not looking for anything, that he just wants to go back to Hender-

sonville and run his own group of locals as well as he can, are taken for cool bargaining.

Accepting congratulations, Art is troubled by the strange array of celebrants. He's used to the J. B. Archers and the Allie Stotzers, though they aren't his favorite people. But what is Vincent Cicero doing here, and the white-on-white-shirt fraternity represented by Tiny Lake and Three Fingers Jones? And the chorus girls from the IBHT's all-star revue? And to compound his confusion and concern, there is George Henderson III, an expansive George Henderson, taking bows because his fortunes have been rising with Joey Hopper's. Mobsters, managers, fixers, politicians, big-league lawyers like "Governor" Thayne Winslow—a strange assembly to be toasting the victory of labor reform over the exposed corruption of Honest Bill Reed.

Like a world's heavyweight champion psychologically keeping his opponent waiting ten minutes before entering the ring, Joey Hopper has delayed his entrance. The band strikes up a lively version of "I'm in Love with a Wonderful Guy."

With a beautifully gowned, orchid-corsaged, and slightly tipsy Paula at his side, Joey struts from group to group accepting plaudits, embraces, kisses, congratulations. When he reaches the puzzled and out-of-place Art Nielsen, he tells him that he should move down to Washington and stop wasting his time in the boondocks. Joey could use him as a personal rep. Art would be useful both as a good-luck charm and as a handy reminder of Joey's rank-and-file origin. Art says thanks, but he has too much to do in Hendersonville; his boys aren't

satisfied with the way the contract with Henderson & Son
is being enforced. There has been some grumbling about
another strike to force George Henderson to live up to his
agreement. Joey tells Art not to worry. Anyway, this is no
night for talking shop. Once he gets in his new office, he
can handle George Henderson easy. Art would like to
pursue this, but Joey moves to join the circle of IBHT
VIPs—Thayne Winslow, Allie Stotzer, J. B. Archer, and
the latest addition, Vincent Cicero, who, thanks to Joey's
support, has become an International vice-president.

Joey gets around to Beverly Lambert, who seems
deeply involved in conversation and champagne with
George Henderson's cool, handsome wife, Ashley. "Well,
Joey, you've got it," Beverly says. "The youngest president
of the biggest union in the world. Where do we go from
here?" Ashley Henderson just eyes him, ungiving, as if
determined to ignore his existence.

"Honey, stick around and see," Joey says, even in
this moment of triumph passing up the trays of cocktails
and champagne to which Beverly and Ashley help themselves liberally. "When these jokers are sleeping off their
hangovers, I'm going to be up at seven with a clear
head."

"If you have any midnight dictation, I'm in 1002,"
Beverly whispers.

"I might, tonight I just might." Joey winks and goes
on to greet other important guests.

"No wonder George calls him The Animal," Ashley
Henderson says in her finishing-school voice. "George

told me quite a lot about him, but he didn't tell me about his eyes."

"I know," Beverly says. "Jay and I have traveled all over the country with him and I'm still afraid to look into his eyes."

"You're mad for him." Ashley sounds petulant.

"Don't be jealous, Ash," Beverly says softly over the rim of her glass. "He works twenty-five hours a day. Even if he were interested, he never has the time."

In the early morning hours, Joey knocks on the door of 1002. Beverly's husky voice invites him in, but on entering he is bewildered to find her naked in bed with Ashley Henderson. The sheets are rumpled but, as Ashley takes a half-smoked joint from Beverly, their poise is intact. "Joey," Beverly says, "I really didn't expect you to drop in."

"All of a sudden I felt I needed some relaxation." For once in his life, he feels confused.

"Don't be bashful, Mr. President," Ashley says. "Join the party."

"Looks like you've already got a party."

Beverly takes a drag. "Don't be so old-fashioned, killer. There are times when two's a crowd and three's a party. Take your shoes off."

This is a different kind of toughness, a different game from the ones Joey knows how to play.

"Have fun, girls. I might still go back to my room and wake up Paula." He backs out lamely.

Ashley Henderson laughs. "Well, at least we made

him blush. That's our evil deed for the day!" She sucks in
the seductive smoke, pours champagne for Beverly, and
hands it to her like an impatient lover.

*The next witness before the Senate Committee is the
quiet, studious Phil Mahoney, who testifies that he and
Dave Edelman had flown out to the Coast for the IBHT
Convention to question, among other people, Vincent
Cicero. For almost a month Cicero had been strangely
elusive. They never had been able to find him in his office
or at his home in Capital City's fashionable Sherwood
Hills section, where his servants and family never seemed
to know where he was or when he might return. So
Mahoney and Edelman had decided to track him down
in Los Angeles.*

*"And did you have any difficulties with Mr. Cicero
when you did catch up with him?" Dennis Crawford asks.*

*"Well, I wouldn't call it exactly a cordial exchange of
ideas. . . ."*

27

What actually happened: Phil Mahoney and Dave
Edelman are admitted to Cicero's suite in the Ambassador by Tiny Lake. Three Fingers Jones is also present.

"You've been a hard man to find," Dave Edelman tells Cicero.

"Look, we're in the middle of an important election. I have to keep moving around."

"Vince, you're due at the Southeast caucus right this second," Tiny cues him. "Well, boys—see you right after the Convention."

"Just in case we miss each other," Mahoney says, "here's a subpoena to appear on the twenty-eighth of this month." He hands it to Cicero.

Tiny Lake grabs the slender Mahoney and begins to rough him up.

"Don't push him, Tiny. I like to avoid trouble," Cicero says.

"We also have a subpoena for you to produce all of your personal records," Phil says coolly, ignoring the mountainous Tiny Lake.

"I told you on the phone, the lawyers are trying to line them up for you," Cicero says. "After all, I'm interested in a dozen different enterprises. You can't expect all those papers overnight."

"It's been nearly three months since we first asked you for them," Dave Edelman reminds him.

"We've been studying the records of your Local 333," Phil Mahoney says. "There are some interesting items. For instance, there's five hundred dollars a week for the Brotherhood Athletic Association. We've been unable to locate any such institution. Then we find that a thousand dollars a week went to pay the training expenses of a heavyweight prizefighter by the name of Georgie Gardner and his manager of record, Willie Banks, who is known as a near and dear friend of Blinky Palermo. But so far this year, the ring earnings of Mr. Gardner, some two hundred thousand dollars, have been split three ways between you, Mr. Banks, and Mr. Hopper. Would you deny that under oath, Mr. Cicero?"

Vincent Cicero is looking into the bureau mirror, fixing his tie and combing the black, wavy hair on which he prides himself. "I haven't got time to answer silly questions. Tiny is right. I've got to get down to the caucus. You stay here and sit on the phone, Tiny."

"Okay, we'll see you in Washington," Dave Edelman says over his chewed cigar.

As soon as Cicero exits, Tiny turns on the two investigators. "Look, you know what this is—inhuman prosecution, pure and simple prosecution. Vincent Cicero is a prince. It breaks my heart to see a man who only wants to do good in the world hounded and prosecuted by government Boy Scouts."

"We don't have to take any abuse from you, Mr. Lake," Dave Edelman says. "I think we already have enough on you to get you indicted for commercial bribery, felonious assault, and perjury."

"I'll felonious you two creeps right here and now," Tiny says. He starts to lean his three hundred pounds against the stocky but considerably shorter Dave Edelman.

"Leave 'em alone," Three Fingers Jones suddenly speaks up. "You heard Vince's orders. Don't cowboy 'em."

Tiny Lake subsides. "Well, it makes my blood boil," he mutters.

"While we are at it, here's your subpoena, Tiny," Phil Mahoney says. "Thanks for your hospitality."

He and Dave exit, leaving Tiny staring at his subpoena. "Shit. Ya try to do a job for the workin' stiff in this
country and this is the thanks ya get for it."

"Put the cryin' towel away," Three Fingers advises
him. "Vince 'n' Joey ain't so stupid dumb like you. They
got the first team behind 'em. The real biggies. The
names you never see in the papers. 'N' they got Thayne
Winslow an' the smartest legal-beagles in the country.
They'll know how t' answer the questions."

*In the Hearing Room the witness is Joey Hopper,
with Thayne Winslow and his sharp-eyed assistant, Lou
Vass, at his side. Dennis Crawford is asking Joey if it is
true that he and Vincent Cicero are partners in a
prizefighter trained and paid at IBHT expense.*

*Joey fields the question as if it were a detail too
petty for his valuable time.* "I think I heard Local 333 had
some sort of Athletic Fund, but our International has almost one thousand locals. You can't expect me to know
what's goin' on in every one of 'em."

"But we have a tape of a telephone call between you
and Vincent Cicero, Mr. Hopper, in which he tells you he
is sending Tiny Lake over with sixty thousand dollars as
your share of Mr. Gardner's purse in a bout at Caesar's
Palace in Las Vegas. Would you like to hear it?"

"Go ahead and play it," *Joey shrugs.* "It won't prove
nothin'. As I remember it, I think maybe Vince made a
bet f'me that night."

"Mr. Santoro's study of your last income-tax return
also shows forty thousand, five hundred and thirty-two
dollars in racetrack winnings. This happens to be exactly

*half the winnings of Mr. Cicero. Mr. Cicero's racing sta-
ble is incorporated under the name of M&P. M happens
to stand for Monique Cicero and P might stand for Paula
Hopper. We believe you are a silent partner in this stable, Mr. Hopper, and that the expenses are paid for out of
union funds."*

*"Look, what Mr. Cicero does with his racing stable is
his business. Once in a while he might give me a tip on
something he's got going and I've been pretty lucky.
That's all I know about it. Any further questions, why
don't you ask Mr. Cicero himself?"*

*Vincent Cicero takes the stand again. Does he have a
prizefighter whom he supports out of union funds and
does he share the profits with Mr. Hopper?*

*"I decline to answer on the grounds that it might
tend to incriminate me."*

*Crawford tries again. "And do union funds, as checks
from Local 333 seem to indicate, also support the M&P
racing stable, in which Mr. Hopper is a silent partner?"*

"I decline to answer . . ."

*In frustration, the chairman, Senator McAllen, asks a
question of his own. "Mr. Cicero, are you associated in
any way, shape, or form with Mr. Joey Hopper?"*

*Vincent Cicero confers in whispers with Thayne
Winslow. Then once more he returns to the same monot-
onous ploy: "I must decline to answer . . ."*

*"You will step aside, Mr. Cicero," the chairman says.
"Mr. Hopper, will you please come around."*

*As Cicero rises, a news photographer moves in to
take his picture. But Vince swings and smashes the cam-
era. Sergeants at arms grab him. The chairman warns
him, "Mr. Cicero, I realize tempers are running high.*

That's understandable when questions are being asked on the basis of months of thorough investigation that could shake a powerful organization to its foundations. But we must have decorum."

"If he has to take my picture, Senator, let 'im take it from the other side so the bum eye won't show," Cicero protests as he is led back to the witness section while Joey Hopper takes his place at the witness microphone under the glare of the TV lights.

The chairman opens up on him: "Mr. Hopper, I believe you were present as a spectator during most of the testimony when your predecessor, General President Bill Reed, chose to take the Fifth Amendment no less than one hundred and forty-six times in answer to questions as to whether or not he had misused union funds. We find your pattern somewhat different. You have not resorted to the Fifth Amendment. Instead you say, 'I don't know, that's George's business, or Mike's, or Tom's'—and then George and Mike and Tom or just now, Mr. Cicero, come before us and in effect take the Fifth Amendment for you by proxy."

Thayne Winslow insists on being heard. "Senator, before I served my great commonwealth as chief executive, I was—as I am today—a devoted student of constitutional law. May I remind you that the privilege of the Bill of Rights is a shield for the innocent as well as the guilty. The fact that a witness comes before this illustrious body and invokes the privilege against self-incrimination should in no way carry an inference of guilt. We are fighting here for basic principles."

Dennis Crawford asks the chairman if he may answer the impassioned ex-Governor. "Mr. Winslow, I don't

*believe any of us need to be lectured on the significance
of the Fifth Amendment. It was written into our Bill of
Rights at the insistence of George Mason of Virginia and
it is one of the vital rights of a free people against the potential abuses of government and star-chamber proceedings. But may I also remind you that the AFL-CIO has
taken a stand against allowing its officers to come before
a public tribunal and refuse to account for their actions
as union stewards? As individuals they certainly have the
right to protect themselves against criminal indictment,
but when we ask a man whether or not he has violated
his trust to his union and he refuses to answer on the
grounds of self-incrimination, isn't it human to expect his
associates to demand an immediate investigation into his
fitness to hold his position of trust? In the one hundred
and seventy-six days of these hearings, nearly three hundred members of the IBHT have told us that an honest
answer would tend to incriminate them. I would now like
to address this question to the new president of the
IBHT: Mr. Hopper, what do you intend to do about
this situation?"*

*"Don't worry," Joey says, "if anyone has done any-
thing wrong in my union, Hopper will look into it.
Hopper will straighten it out."*

*Dennis Crawford answers, "Mr. Hopper, we do
worry. We worry for the American people and the decent
labor movement in the United States. You have just won
an election on a reform platform after this Committee
brought to light an alarming record of grand larceny for
which your predecessor in office will undoubtedly be indicted—yes, the same man for whom you finessed a cushy
pension at the recent Convention. And in your own area*

you have not kept the hoodlums out—on the contrary, you seem to be opening the doors to them wider than ever."

"If you're so sure of that, it oughta be proved in a court of law like Governor Winslow says," Joey answers.

Senator McAllen says: "Mr. Hopper, this extended session is coming to an end. But it is only fair to warn you that a considerable staff under the direction of our able chief counsel will continue to investigate your organization, as well as others, both in labor and management, which are suspected of defrauding their members and the public. Meanwhile, I am sure every one of my colleagues on this Committee joins me in urging you to live up to your tremendous responsibilities."

Joey Hopper gives it back to the Committee in the third-person singular. "Nobody has to lecture Hopper on how to do his job. I don't need the AFL-CIO on one side or any labor-baiting Senators on the other giving me lectures on responsibilities. Hopper will take care of Hopper and the IBHT."

Dennis Crawford says, "Mr. Chairman, we have no further questions at this time. We would like to take Mr. Hopper at his word that he will take the proper steps to clean up the unhealthy situation in his International Union. Ex-Governor Winslow has done his eloquent best to associate Joey Hopper with the fight for human rights, almost as if taking the Fifth Amendment had become a patriotic duty, but we believe that testimony here—seven weeks, five hundred witnesses, and seventeen thousand pages of it—has developed a pattern of abuse indicating that the fundamental human rights of union members are being trampled on. The corruption breeds corruption, the

*violence breeds violence. In the months ahead we intend
to investigate this spreading cancer with every ounce of
our strength and resources."*

*The chairman thanks Chief Counsel Crawford and
his staff for their diligent efforts. Further hearings on the
IBHT will be called when Mr. Crawford and his investigators have developed sufficient additional material.
Meanwhile, Mr. Hopper may stand aside*

*Joey Hopper, unfazed, unreconstructed, standing
bigger than ever in his shoes, winks brazenly at young
Crawford. "Good luck, Denny Boy." He swaggers out
with his constitutional expert, Thayne Winslow, and his
admiring henchmen.*

*As the Hearing Room empties, Crawford shakes his
head.*

*"Where do we go from here, Pops?" Charley Walker
asks.*

*"Back to the salt mines," Crawford says, chewing on
his pencil.*

In the Hot Potato, a teenage jukebox hangout in Hendersonville, Tommy Nielsen is disco-dancing with his favorite date. On the small, crowded floor other high-school

couples are improvising wildly. Suddenly an ax smashes into the jukebox, almost cracking it in two. Wielding the ax is Tiny Lake, accompanied by Three Fingers Jones.

Stunned, but Muscle Hollow tough, Tommy Nielsen wants to know what's going down.

"You're a union kid," Tiny says. "You know the score. That machine don't have no union label on it. I warned this bum on the phone"—he thumbs toward the terrified proprietor—"if he didn't pull the plug, we'd have to enforce the union regulation."

Two of Tiny Lake's corporals carry in another jukebox. Tiny points to the prominent label on its side, *Local 1223*.

"I know all the locals in Uncle Art's area. I never heard of any 1223," Tommy talks back.

"Kid, if you and your little girl friend wanna do any more dancin' around here, you're gonna do it to the music of 1223," Tony says.

Then he turns on the tavern-keeper, "Use any more scab machines 'n' next time we'll put the ax in your head insteada the box."

Young Tommy watches as the goons drag out the smashed "nonunion" record machine while the owner looks on helplessly.

An all-night diner, a favorite coffee-break spot for drivers on the outskirts of Hendersonville, with a flamboyant sign, "Truckers Welcome," is being picketed by Tiny Lake and his enforcers with placards reading, TURNER'S DINER UNFAIR TO ORGANIZED LABOR, LOCAL 1223, IBHT.

Alerted by Tommy, Art Nielsen drives up with Deac

Johnson in his old car to find out what is going on. No strike can be called in this area unless it is voted on by the Joint Council, whose officers happen to be Art Nielsen and Deac Johnson. This so-called strike of so-called Local 1223 is illegal.

"It is like hell," says Tiny Lake.

"We wanna see the charter."

"Charter-shmarter—I got half-a-dozen charters, wise guy," Tiny says.

"Who are the officers?" Art wants to know.

"You're lookin' at the president of 1223," Tiny Lake says. "Jones here is president of 1224, Henry Mingus is president of 1225 . . ."

"Harry the Horse, who's got a lock on the vending machines in Capital City?" Art asks incredulously.

"Watch your language, Brother Nielsen," says Tiny Lake. "So okay, you nominated our General President, that doesn't make you God Almighty."

"Who are the other officers?" Art persists.

"Secretary-treasurer of 1223 is Sam Cristoli. Secretary-treasurer of 1224 is Roland Bender."

"Champ Cristoli? Bugsy Bender? They've got records as long as your own, Tiny. We run decent unions up here."

"Brother Nielsen, you and me are fellow members of the IBHT," Tiny says in the righteous tone he often uses. "I think you should welcome new locals into your area."

"I want to see those charters," Art says.

"You'll see 'em when you see 'em."

"Meanwhile my petroleum drivers aren't going to respect this phony picket line," Art says. "This is no strike—it's a shakedown."

"Brother Nielsen," Tiny scolds, "if it wasn't you were such an old friend of our beloved president, Joey Hopper, I'd give you a massage that would take a few pounds off you and I wouldn't charge you a cent—them services I offer free, gratis, to union brothers."

A petroleum truck drives up and Porky Porcovich and Billy Kasco climb down from the cab, on their way into Pop Turner's for coffee.

"On strike—you guys don't look like scabs," Tiny shouts.

"What goes here?" Billy Kasco asks.

"Go on through, Billy, this strike is a three-dollar bill," Art says.

Billy and Porky nervously pass through the goon picket line.

"Brother Nielsen, you're a disgrace to organized labor," Tiny Lake says.

"I'm labor three generations back," Art bristles. "There never was a scab in the Nielsen family. You better pull your bums out of here."

A couple of Tiny's boys make a move for Art. "Let 'im go, boys," Tiny says magnanimously. "I got faith in the International. Vinnie C. will straighten 'im out."

A few weeks later, Art parks his car in his driveway and walks around to the small backyard where his little son, Joey, is in his playpen. He picks the child up, giving him a piggyback right to the back door and into the kitchen. Edna is preparing supper. She sees Art is troubled. Something wrong? Oh, just some union problems, he tries to brush it off. His day isn't over, she says. Some men have come up from Washington to see him. They're waiting in the parlor.

Art goes to find Dave Edelman and Phil Mahoney. They show him their credentials. They have come to investigate the jukebox racket that is spreading all over the state. Apparently Vincent Cicero is using the IBHT union label to force his machines into every possible location. As far as they have been able to find out, the locals under Art Nielsen's leadership are clean. But what can he tell them about the underworld element moving in on him under the banner of the IBHT?

Art says they aren't telling him anything he doesn't know. He's bucking the invasion of shadow locals run out of Tiny Lake's pocket, like this Local 1223. But he's been raised to believe that labor should clean its own house. Congressional interference in labor disputes is bad news.

Dave Edelman says they are here to study his dispute—as he calls it—with these jukebox locals. Their boss, Chief Counsel Dennis Crawford, is convinced that it will take two forces, honest labor and thorough government investigation, to do the job.

"You're free to investigate all you want, you can look at our books. I know Deac Johnson, our treasurer, is one hundred percent," Art says. "But I've got to handle this problem my own way, inside the movement."

30

Art calls a meeting of his Joint Council. He expects several hundred in the humble hall that is now part of their expanding but basically proletarian operation. To Art's dismay, the hall is packed with Tiny Lake's jukebox-local pistoleros. As soon as Art enters with his father, Deac Johnson, and young Tommy, he sees that the one-armed-bandit crowd is on hand. Along with Tiny and Three Fingers Jones are Harry the Horse Mingus, Bugsy Bender, Champ Cristoli, and other motley brothers.

As chairman, Art challenges the right of these new

members to attend the Council meeting. Tiny gets up
with the charters—the International has attached them to
the Henderson County Council. As a result he moves that
Art Nielsen be suspended from office on the grounds that
he failed to support the strike of Local 1223. Three
Fingers promptly seconds the motion.

"Even if you've got a piece of paper, there is no
Local 1223," Art fights back. "I defy you to show me your
membership list. All you've got is some phony charters
and a bunch of musclemen masquerading as union
officers."

"There is a motion before this house," shouts Tiny
Lake. "You got to call for a vote."

"We do like hell!" says Billy Kasco.

The meeting breaks up in a chair-smashing wrestling
match. . . .

An hour later, a skull session of Art's backers is held
in the Nielsen kitchen, with the worried Edna serving
them coffee: Art, Deac, Porky, Billy, and a few other
loyal drivers, with Tommy silently taking it all in. They
have got to do something fast, Art urges. Otherwise they
won't have a union any more—at least not the kind of
genuine trade union they started way back with Local
101.

There is only one thing to do, Art decides, go down
to Washington and talk to Joey Hopper personally. Joey
is so busy with nationwide negotiations these days he obviously doesn't know how these jukebox and pinball artists are using and destroying the good name of the IBHT.

Art's group agrees it's a swell idea. Art says he'll start

driving down to Washington tonight. Billy Kasco thinks he ought to fly. That way he can see Joey in the morning. It's pretty expensive, Art says, he doesn't like to dip into the treasury they've been carefully nursing All the boys say they will chip in. Even Tommy wants to put up five collars he's saved from his paper route. "I figger we're fighting for my old man," he says. "These cowbcys would put him back in his grave all over again."

31

*I*n Washington, Art Nielsen approaches the resplendent IBHT Headquarters Building, with its magnificent glass and marble front and impressive inscription: "The Wheels of America—A Public Trust."

Inside, Art is awed by the hundred-foot main lobby, walled and floored in dark and light marble. Through the bronze doorway he can look across the park to the white dome of the nation's Capitol. Facing the main entrance is a brisk, attractive receptionist. Does Mr. Nielsen have an appointment? If he will wait a moment, she will check with Mr. Hopper's secretary. Art looks around the multimillion-dollar lobby with its modern leather couches and its stately columns faced with tile mosaic. Staring back at Art is an enormous photomural of International General President Joey Hopper, an extension of the huge poster Tiny Lake carried at the Convention, with the various heroic captions: *Son of a Labor Martyr; From Crackle Crates to Petroleum Tankers; Youngest General President in IBHT History.* It is an overpowering photograph of the grinning, triumphant Joey Hopper, similar to the 8 by 10 in Art's small office in Hendersonville.

The receptionist tells Art he may go up and points to the first of a bank of elevators. Soon he is in General President Joey Hopper's outer office. A gray-haired, dignified executive secretary buzzes Mr. Hopper—a moment later, a mahogany door slides open and Art finds himself in Joey's enormous, cypress-paneled, leather-and-walnut-furnished, soundproof office.

Joey is talking on one of his many phones, but beckons Art in. The performance is impressive. In his brisk, terse, impatiently efficient fashion, Joey is handling union problems from coast to coast.

"Listen, Ben, don't give me any crap about New England—I know the agreement by heart—forty hours for first-class riggers is three hundred 'n' forty-five sixty— okay, don't argue with me—enforce it!"

Joey hangs up. No time for good-byes. An intercom rasps: Denver on three. Joey grabs another phone. "Jack —don't give me any shit about calling a strike out there— just insist on five twenty-three for second-shift work and if they don't like it, they can shove it. And if they won't shove it, let 'em call me." There is a brief pause for Denver's answer, but Joey cuts him off. "Tough! Call me back 'n' lemme know."

At last he has a moment to embrace Art, and it is a big, warm hello. Then another phone call—"Listen, Thayne, I read the subpoena—ya mean t' tell me those bastards across the park have a right to pick up all our personal and confidential letters and interoffice memos? Well, you're supposed t' be a constitutional lawyer, goddammit—so act like one. Call me back. And I don't want no wishy-washy alibis!"

He hangs up. "Jeez, the stupidities I got to put up with. How's Edna? How's the little slugger? Swell. Now what's your problem?"

Awed by Joey's high and mighty office and his stepped-up tempo, Art gives his old friend a brief run-down on the plight of the Hendersonville-based Joint Council. This jukebox setup is a mockery of everything they started, and it's getting so out of hand that only Joey can handle it.

Joey sounds concerned and sympathetic. He certainly doesn't want hoods and undesirable elements moving in on good old Hendersonville. He appreciates the fact that Art is bringing it to his attention. Now he's got an emergency meeting with the southern area over-the-road boys. Why doesn't he come to supper tonight at Joey's suite in the Shoreham? It'll give 'em more chance to talk—and Paula, who's up from Capital City on a shopping trip, would love to see him anyway.

On the way out, Art passes the open door of the reception room of J. B. Archer and notices Beverly Lambert.

"Welcome to Taj Mahal," says Beverly.

"I thought by this time you'd be the president's executive secretary," Art says.

"You should know our president better than that," Beverly says. "The first thing he did was move Bill Reed's little blonde out and take in Mrs. Beecher, the widow of a driver killed in an accident. Our president never misses a trick."

"He sure seems to be doing a great job," Art says, looking up at the large-size picture of Joey Hopper that dominates this office also. The famous, cocky Joey Hopper smile seems to be everywhere.

"J for Justice, T for Tough, H for—well, I'm too much of a lady to tell you what I think the H is for," Beverly says. "Now that you know where our little tepee is located, don't be a stranger. It does our hearts good to see an honest-to-God workingman once in a while."

32

That evening, Art goes to the Hopper suite at the Shoreham, hoping to have a chance over supper to explain his troubles in detail. But Joey rushes in, full of hurry and four-letter words. Shit, Art will have to excuse him but he has to dash off to a summit meeting at Allie

Stotzer's, with Thayne Winslow and a bunch of lawyers. That asshole Crawford and his motherfucker blood-hounds are on his neck again, making all kinds of impos-sible requests for documents, bank accounts, and all the rest of that crap. Thayne Winslow and those other genius lawyers of his have to get busy running the ends. He's gonna give it to Thayne but good tonight. The old crook is on a hundred-and-fifty-thousand-dollar retainer—and he'd better start earning it!

Off Joey runs into the night, leaving Paula and Art alone for the first time in years. Paula brings out a bottle. She says she only drinks beer when Joey's in town, be-cause he cuffs her around for boozing, but she has some bottles cached for when he's away, which is most of the time.

But you haven't changed too much, Art says. She's still an awful pretty kid.

"Look, we're old steadies, we used t' go out under the bridge after the Saturday night dances—you don't have to lie to me," Paula says. "I've put on twenty pounds, remember that cute little figure I useta have, 36-22-34? Now it's 40-40-40. The mirror tells me the truth. And of course the Almighty Hopper."

"You still love Joey?" Art asks.

Paula drinks and strokes one of her cats. "Love? It's like loving a Sherman tank. I got the tractor treads all over me."

It's a hard moment for Art. Whenever he's close to Paula, even a disenchanted, fleshier Paula, she's still the woman he's always wanted.

All he can think to say is, "I'm sorry, Paula."

"Don't be. If there's anything I can't stand it's you bein' sorry for me. And probably thinkin' how much better off I'd be if I hadn't run out on you. Art, I couldn't help it. Joey had me fascinated like a snake."

Hell, Art says, it's no bed of roses back in Hendersonville. He's up to his neck in troubles, too. "Edna's been breaking out in hives, she's so scared of these muscle-boy 'unionists' who've been moving into our neck of the woods."

Paula warns Art to be careful. She's become friends with Vincent Cicero's wife, Monique—joins her in her box at the track quite often. She sees the kind of trash that shows up at Cicero's, even though he himself is a perfect gentleman and devoted to his family. But she's heard some things. Art better keep his back covered.

It's funny, he says ruefully over his drink, it used to be that we had to be careful about standing up too strong to the bosses. It's a sad day when we have to be careful about standing up to our union brothers.

"Brothers," Paula says, downing her drink. "Don't tell Joey I said so, but you meet some pretty funny brothers in this IB."

"What time you think he'll be back?"

Paula shrugs. "Who knows? Maybe not until breakfast. And I don't even think it's other women—lots of times he goes back to the office and works all night. Art, I sleep in the same bed with 'im and he's more of a stranger now than when I first fell for 'im. So don't ask me what time he'll get back. Don't even ask me what he's doing."

She starts to sob. Art puts his arms around her.

"You'd better go." She draws away from him. "I'm fond of you and I'm lonely and I love my sister Eddie. You'd better go, Art. Good luck with the gorillas. . . ."

33

When Art Nielsen returns to his Joint Council office in Hendersonville, he opens the door and finds—instead of the friendly faces of Deac Johnson, Porky, and his other officers—Tiny Lake, Three Fingers Jones, Harry the Horse, Bugsy Bender, Champ Cristoli, and other members of the "rival faction."

"That happens to be my desk you're sitting at," Art says.

"Use t' be." Tiny Lake leans back in the revolving chair that creaks under his weight. "I'm the new president of the Council. We had a new election, the same day you left."

"I talked to Joey personally—he's on my side," Art says. The other jukebox-local officers are forming a circle around him.

"Joey called Vinnie C. thirty seconds after you left

the office," Tiny says. "He says you were just a tourist in Washington. Ya just came down to admire the view of our national Capitol from the top floor."

"That isn't what Joey told me," Art says. The coin-box element is breathing on him.

"He's calling our president a liar," Tiny says. "We don't go for that, brother. Show 'im to the elevator, boys."

The jukebox half-dozen, followed by Tiny, crowd Art into the corridor. A few of them slip on brass knuckles. They push him into the elevator and crowd in after him, until he is sardined in the middle. The door closes and the elevator starts down. The arrow on the indicator above the elevator door tells the story of what's happening inside. There is a scream from Art—and another—the sound of scuffling and heavy blows. The screams become fainter as the elevator descends to the main floor—then begin to increase in volume as the arrow points from first to second to third floor again. And then down once more as the working-over continues.

At the ground-floor level, the elevator door opens and the half-dozen musclemen hurry out—leaving the bloody, groin-kicked, face-smashed Art Nielsen in the fetal position on the floor.

Alone on the top floor, Three Fingers Jones pushes the button to bring the elevator up again. Then he calmly heads for the stairs, while the elevator slowly ascends with its unconscious passenger.

In the middle of the night, Paula is alone in the double bed in their house in Capital City, reading *True Romance*, a bottle of ale on the night table, her Siamese cats curled up on the pillows beside her. There are four of them now: Duke and Duchess have had progeny, Prince and Princess.

The phone rings—long-distance from Edna, from the hospital in Hendersonville. She sobs out the news. Art has had his nose and several ribs broken, a number of teeth knocked out. Paula screams, "Oh Christ, no!" Edna's voice is toneless. It's hopeless, maybe fatal she feels, for Art to fight the situation in Hendersonville any longer. When he recovers, what about taking Joey up on his offer at the Convention, to make Art one of his personal reps headquartered in Washington? Paula promises. Joey is off in Houston at a Southwest freight meeting, but as soon as he returns she'll get him to okay the transfer—this she guarantees. Edna can count on the move, the minute Art is strong enough to travel.

Paula finds a charming suburban house in Reston, Virginia, for the Art Nielsen family. She is on the front porch waiting for them when Art drives up in their old car. Edna and the children—Little Joey, almost two now, and an infant daughter, Florrie—are excited by these new, much improved surroundings. Compared to what they had in Hendersonville, it is a mansion—three bedrooms, so Joey won't have to share one with his baby sister. And a lovely lawn and swings and slides that Paula has thoughtfully set up in the backyard. In fact, Paula has even hired a maid for them. On Art's new salary of $30,000 a year, plus expenses and a union car, they can begin to live a little. Little Joey is already swooping happily down the slide. And Edna is practically in tears as she embraces Paula—the kitchen is a modern dream.

"I wish you had done this a year ago, before all that trouble started," Paula says.

Only Art is restrained. Yes, it certainly is a nice house. Yes, the kids and Eddie are certainly going to love it. He and Edna are grateful to her. Only—

His explanation is faltering. He can't help feeling he has let the boys down in leaving Hendersonville. Deac, Porky, the old crowd, are sick about what happened to the union they formed and were so proud of.

"But as an assistant to the president, maybe you can do more good down here," Paula tries to encourage him.

"Well, maybe I can. I sure hope so." Perhaps, being closer to the throne here at headquarters, he'll be able to open Joey's eyes to what Vincent Cicero and his pistoleros are doing to their union. But there isn't complete conviction in what Art says as he takes over his new, middle-class home. He still limps and has to favor his left side where the ribs were stove in. The nightmare elevator ride has taken a piece out of him.

35

In the cluttered offices of the Investigating Committee in the Old Senate Office Building, with files piled high on his desk and charts on the walls, in an atmosphere of intense activity, Dennis Crawford is preparing for the new hearings. They are concentrating on the coin-machine operations multiplying through the country, thanks to the IBHT-underworld alliance. A map with pins on the wall behind Crawford's desk reflects the geographical spread of this billion-dollar, union-fronted racket.

Dave Edelman and Phil Mahoney come in to report an interesting development. Art Nielsen has been run out of his own Joint Council area by the coin-machine "paper-local" racketeers. He refused to back down to them and received a near-fatal working-over for his trouble. But he's a strange case, because he is obviously tied in with Joey Hopper, both through marriage, since they are brothers-in-law, and through their original Local 101 camaraderie.

Crawford urges Edelman and Mahoney to keep after Art. An honest trade unionist, a deeply involved member of the IBHT, and a personal friend of Joey Hopper could be a big plus for them—if they could only get him to talk.

As Dave and Phil leave, Charley Walker hurries in with another team of investigators. Art's is no isolated case. Investigations are going on in Cleveland, Miami, Seattle, Chicago. . . . The coin-box racket is as big a bonanza for the mob as booze was in the twenties—only camouflaged with respectability. The vending-machine bosses, unlike the bootleggers, aren't naked Al Capones but "union leaders" like Vincent Cicero, with an invisible empire of *capos* and their respectable friends behind them.

So Dave and Phil come to see Art Nielsen in his new modern office at IBHT headquarters. Art looks tamed and middle-classed. His office is not large, but, like Joey Hopper's, it is cypress-paneled, with handsome leather chairs. Art's feeling is that he hasn't sold out but is working to do what he can to improve conditions within the system. Like J. B. Archer on a higher level, Art still clings to the hope that Joey Hopper, once he has all the power he needs or hungers for, will "throw the bums out."

Dave and Phil tell Art they are continuing the investigation they discussed with him in Hendersonville. They realize that since that time he has been the victim of union-racketeer violence. Has his silence been bought off by this cushy job in Washington? They tell him they are not issuing him a subpoena. But at the next hearings,

Dennis Crawford may ask him to describe Chapter Two of the Hendersonville story, since it seems to typify the intimidation being directed against decent IBHT local leaders in various parts of the country.

Art is wary of these government snoops. As a personal assistant to President Hopper, he feels it would not be right for him to answer their questions, even informally, until he has had an opportunity to discuss the matter with Joey. But whatever abuses may be committed by unscrupulous men misusing the IBHT label in outlying areas, he is sure that Hopper remains the same militant labor leader he himself nominated at the Convention.

Dave and Phil are professionally cordial. They hope Art is right. But, since he suffered so directly at the hands of Tiny Lake and the paper-local mob, whose guiding genius is obviously Vincent Cicero—they will undoubtedly have to talk to him again.

As soon as they leave, Art hurries up to Joey Hopper's office.

He finds Joey in a strategy meeting with Thayne Winslow and Lou Vass, Allie Stotzer, J. B. Archer, and Beverly Lambert.

Joey is in a fury. So Dennis Crawford thinks he's hitting pay dirt with this national investigation of the jukebox racket? And Thayne is worried that Crawford's staff may have stumbled on a vulnerable area? Joey is fed up with Thayne's worries. At his first meeting with Winslow, Joey had treated the Governor with the respect due from a parvenu. Now he treats Winslow more like an office boy. The IBHT has no vulnerable areas; *that* is the idea "the Governor" has to pound into the heads of those nippleheads twenty-four hours a day. Joey does all the talking. They do all the listening.

When Art comes in with his tale of the Edelman-Mahoney probe, Stotzer reacts with deep concern. Crawford has learned a lot since the first hearings. Sometimes a chief counsel is discouraged when he doesn't score a knockout in the first round. But Denny Crawford doesn't seem to be hunting just for headlines, like some other congressional committees. He really seems determined to get to the bottom of the troubles in the IBHT.

Hopper won't allow a single defeatist word. What troubles? Haven't they picked up 300,000 new members in the last twelve months? Doesn't their percent-per-hour wage increase top every other union's in America? He points to elaborate Madison-Avenue-style charts illustrating his progress.

Just the same, Allie Stotzer—in his fancy new Tareyton vest and tasseled Gucci shoes—thinks Joey should not underrate Dennis Crawford. The chief counsel is a more tenacious opponent than Allie had anticipated. Thayne Winslow agrees, but maybe he can use some of his connections to head him off. He thinks young Crawford is looking ahead to bigger things. Maybe Winslow can bring certain influences to bear to suggest that if Crawford continues his present uncompromising course, he may as well kiss his political ambitions good-bye.

It's obvious to Winslow, he pontificates, that Crawford is driven by personal ambition and is using this televised investigation as a stepping stone to elective office. Some say old Senator McAllen is ready to retire and throw his support to his brash young protégé. Hell, this

Crawford kid has money, looks, brains, guts—the arrogant little bastard could make a run at the White House one of these days if they don't stop him soon.

Joey listens. Okay, fine, let Thayne Winslow work the high road, as he calls it. And stick it to Denny Boy good. Meanwhile, Allie Stotzer will shift his public-relations organization into high gear, present this Senate Committee attack on Joey Hopper as the opening gun of a congressional campaign against all organized labor. Let J.B. write a good, strong statement for him about the economic and social gains by Joey Hopper in behalf of his one and a quarter million members.

But there is also a low road, Joey reminds them. While Winslow is working the Hill, and Stotzer is spending to the best advantage some of that three million dollars the IBHT has allocated for public relations—call that the middle road—there's a job on the low road for his old sidekick, Art Nielsen.

Art is concerned. What could he possibly do on a par with the contributions of wheeler-dealers like Governor Winslow, Allie Stotzer, and J. B. Archer?

Joey's answer is startling: Art can pretend to cooperate with Dennis Crawford's investigators.

"You mean you want me to spy on the Committee?" Art asks.

"This is war," Joey says. Every army uses advance scouts who penetrate the enemy lines and come back and report troop dispositions and plans. "You just happen to be in a beautiful spot to do that, Art. Tiny Lake and his Boy Scouts knocked you out of the box in Hendersonville.

You got the shit beat out of you. Hell, that's why Crawford's punks came to you."

"I didn't tell them anything, Joey," Art says.

"I know that, Art, I trust you," Joey says. "Also,
every office in this building is bugged." He reveals a hidden panel. "I flip a switch and I'm in your office. A good
executive has to know what's going on, right?"

The feelings of Joey's confreres are mixed; they don't
dare be critical, they are too awed and bullied—and
trapped. All of these men who began with some dignity,
some sense of power, intelligence, or authority greater
than Joey Hopper's, have been reduced to puppets, silently ashamed.

"So," Joey pushes his latest idea, "all you have to do
is call one of Crawford's boys—no, better call Denny himself—and tell him you've been thinking over Dave and
Phil's suggestion and decided to cooperate, to help them
lick this terrible jukebox racket."

Art resists the idea. Sure he's hurt, he's confused, he's
hoping to get Joey to do something about the disgraceful
state of affairs since Cicero moved his boys into their old
Joint Council. But he isn't a private-eye type. He can't
see himself going in and spying on the Senate Committee
staff—even for Joey Hopper.

Joey is still able to wield over Art the persuasive
power he had on him in the days when Local 101 was
under fire; when he and Joey saw eye to eye on ends,
although Art objected to some of the violent, direct-action
means. Joey senses this and is quick to use it. Hell, if it
wasn't for the two of 'em, Joey reminds Art, the petroleum
drivers of Henderson County would still be on the short

end of the open shop. Now he and Art are united again, on
a national level. This Senate Committee pretending to
"cleanse" or "reform" labor is just Henderson, Sr., on a
nationwide instead of a county scale. Dennis Crawford
is nothing but a young phony out to make a name for
himself by breaking the back of the IBHT. It's a more
complex fight, more subtle than picketing Old Man
Henderson. But if Art can ingratiate himself with Crawford and his staff, and find out what their next moves are
—he'll be doing more for organized labor than he ever did
in Hendersonville. And in return, Joey promises to get
Vincent Cicero and Tiny Lake to lay off their old local—
he promises it will be returned to the democratic leadership of Deac Johnson, Porky Porcovich, Billy Kasco, and
the other charter members of 101.

36

*D*ave Edelman and Phil Mahoney are reporting their
failure to Dennis Crawford in the cluttered suite in the
Old Senate Office Building—Crawford literally up to his
bare elbows in reports from all over the country on the
IBHT coin-box racket and its tie-up with leading
mobsters from Miami to Seattle.

Phil and Dave did their best with Art Nielsen, they say, but they weren't able to dent his loyalty to Joey Hopper. Just then a phone rings. Someone wants to talk to Mr. Crawford. He is calling from a phone booth. He won't say who he is. But he is ready to meet Crawford and he thinks he has a story for him. From a phone booth? Crawford's hunch is proved right—it is Art Nielsen, nervous, unsure of himself.

Crawford tells Art to meet him at his Maryland home that evening. And he instructs Dave and Phil to be there too, but downstairs in the rumpus room, out of sight. Crawford will want a strategy conference once he finds out what Art is really up to.

Art meets Dennis that night in the den of the sprawling Crawford home. It is a wary, sparring session. Art says he has been a victim of mob violence in Hendersonville and that to get even with Vincent Cicero, he wants to help the Committee. Crawford says they have a beautiful file on Cicero and are ready to prove how his "paper" charters are corrupting honest union setups like the one Art was trying to run. His firsthand information could be of great help to the Committee in the next session of hearings. Art, unhappily, says he will try to help; at the same time Crawford senses that Art is trying to milk him for information on exactly how much they have on the IBHT. Deciding finally to give Art a chance to prove himself either way, Crawford tells him to keep in touch, using the code name "Pete Smith" for their mutual protection.

After Art leaves, Dennis joins his assistants downstairs in the rumpus room, with Jan, who has made coffee.
She is as involved in this cause as the rest of them; the
crusade against the labor racketeers has knit them into a
family. What did Dennis think of Art Nielsen? He still
isn't sure. It could be a desperate Hopper ploy to learn
what the line of questioning will be at the next hearings.
Yet there is something honest, even touching, about Nielsen, Dennis feels. He still shows the effects of the terrible
beating he took in the elevator in Hendersonville. His
rage at the Cicero-Lake take-over seems genuine. They
should play him very carefully, not giving him any information that Hopper and his brain trust don't already
know the Committee knows. Dennis has been intuitive
enough to sense that, at heart, Nielsen is a decent man,
an honest trade unionist.

At the same time, Jan points out, he is a personal assistant to Joey Hopper and one of his oldest associates.

They all agree—not to trust Art Nielsen but to try to
use him.

In the kitchen of the Nielsens' Reston home, there is
a counterpoint discussion. Edna gets up in her night-robe
to prepare a bottle for Florrie, and finds Art drinking a
beer.

"Honey, know what time it is? What's the matter?"

"Joey told me not to tell anybody. Not even you. But
I've been to see Denny Crawford." He tells her why.

Crawford! Is he really as arrogant and opinionated as
Joey says?

Art doesn't know. Crawford seemed pretty quiet, he's a good listener, not as driving and ruthless as he had expected. Still Art has to be awfully careful. They say young Crawford hopes to use these hearings as a stepping-stone toward a career in national politics—and Art isn't anxious to be one of the stones. Actually, he wishes Joey had never pushed him into becoming a "double agent." "It's kind of a dangerous road, Eddie. I don't know what's at the end of it."

Edna urges him to come to bed. "You look beat, honey. You gotta get some sleep."

"Yeah, after a while. Just let me sit here and think some more."

37

*L*ate that same night, George Henderson III is alone in his Washington offices—a new modern suite that mirrors the growing national importance of Henderson & Son, thanks to the "sweetheart" contracts he enjoys with Joey Hopper. George has expanded physically, psychologically —everything about him reflects the gains he has achieved through his pragmatic approach to labor-union opportunism. Joey's enforcement of tougher contracts with

Henderson competitors has enabled George to swallow up many of them and become one of the Big Three. Henderson & Son is not only a petroleum company, with refineries and its own tankers in the Gulf of Mexico—it is taxi companies, gas-station chains, over-the-road trucking. George's foresight in sensing the potential in Joey Hopper has given him the Midas touch.

There is a disconcerting knock at his private door. Dave Edelman and Phil Mahoney are here to see him— with a subpoena covering all his correspondence with Joey Hopper. They also have a subpoena for his chief accountant, Henry Nettles. They are interested to learn why Mr. Nettles serves as accountant both for Henderson & Son and for a number of companies apparently owned by the wives of Joey Hopper and Vincent Cicero.

George maintains his aplomb. He doesn't quite see why the government should be hounding respectable businessmen, particularly at this hour of the night. Naturally, the correspondence they seek can't be delivered willy-nilly—he will have to consult his lawyers, his secretaries. But of course he will be willing to cooperate, if given sufficient time.

Dave and Phil are equally "cooperative." They will call again in a week or so.

As soon as the investigators leave, George hurries down the hall to Henry Nettles' office, its door bare of any identification. Nettles is a nonentity, just a conscientious accountant who knows his job—and who never dreamed it would lead him into conflict with the law. George orders Nettles to destroy all incriminating mem-

oranda, contracts, and correspondence. And then to disappear out of the country before Crawford's staff can
serve him with a subpoena. A trapped little man, he is
being drawn into a pattern of defiance of national authority. He is trembling as George leaves him to his all-night
assignment.

Early next morning, Nettles goes to George Henderson, Sr., the aging Chairman of the Board, the man who
first hired him, forty years ago. Conflicted and desperate,
Nettles begs for advice.

Henderson, Sr., is outraged, he tells his son. To be
sure, he has seen Henderson & Son prosper and expand
beyond even his own ambitious dreams. But he has also
seen Joey Hopper grow into a national menace able to
dictate to the entire world of transportation. He has seen
this scoundrel Hopper lead his son across the border of
business respectability into the shadows of criminality.
Nettles has told him of George's order to destroy company records the Senate Committee is seeking under
official subpoena.

George still thinks he can handle his father. "Sir,
Joey and I have an agreement about this. If it ever came
to a showdown with this damnable Dennis Crawford—a
traitor to his class, by the way—I was to destroy certain
records. That is the way the power game has to be
played, Father."

"I am sick of your power game," Henderson, Sr.,
says. "All right, I was a diehard against all unions. And
you saw the potential of using a union—a corruptible

union—to your own advantage. But I tell you right now, I would rather deal with an honest union—even God forbid a militant union—than become a partner of crooks."

"Father, *crook* is one of your old-fashioned concepts," George III says. "This isn't an age of ethics. It's the age of big muscle and big bucks, and what works is what's right. That's what I saw in Joey Hopper. That's why Henderson & Son is now on the New York Stock Exchange and is worth fifteen times what it was when I took over. You came in a millionaire, you may go out a billionaire."

"Son," the old man says, "in the eighty-year history of Henderson & Son this is the first time our government has ever treated us as outlaws, as enemies of the Republic. If you dare burn the records I ordered Nettles not to, I am going to do to you what I'll never forgive you for doing to me—I'll denounce you to the Board of Directors and demand your resignation. Think it over, Mr. President."

Late one night, Art Nielsen goes to Dennis Crawford's suite in the Old Senate Office Building, using the name "Pete Smith" to pass the guards.

Art finds Crawford working hard at his desk, tie pulled loose, sleeves rolled up, going over reports as he prepares his questions for the forthcoming hearings. Pushed to one side of the desk are a half-eaten chicken sandwich and a container of coffee. The weary Sal Santoro comes in for a moment—he's run across some odd endorsements on bank checks that it might be difficult for George Henderson to explain. Crawford says good, he'll discuss it with Sal in a few minutes.

Something about all this late-night activity, the endless pile of papers, reports, and checks that they are processing, the intensity with which they are working, puts new pressure on Art's conscience.

Crawford offers to share the lukewarm coffee, and over the cluttered desk they have their first real talk. Does Crawford mind if Art asks him a question? Not at all, says Crawford. Art hesitates. It's no secret that Crawford is from a wealthy family, he's had all the advantages —but this is now the early hours of Saturday morning. Why is he working so hard? What is he really after?

"Maybe the same thing you're after," Crawford says, munching on the sandwich. "I'm for honest unions. I'm for honest American institutions, whether it's labor or capital. We need them both—but we need them honest. And the only way I can see to keep them honest is to keep digging into them, looking at their books, checking the backgrounds of their officers—we know, for instance, and in the next hearings we think we're going to prove, that the leadership of the IBHT is rotten. Not the poor drivers and warehousemen who pay the ten or fifteen bucks dues a month—and okay, they get some benefits—

I'm talking about the big boys, from President Hopper down. And Art, if they're rotten, if they're crooked, if they play footsie with employers and mobsters—it's just one more crack in the whole society.

"My wife, Jan, kids me because I'm hipped on Roman history—but I tell you the great Roman Republic had its Joey Hoppers and its Vincent Ciceros and its George Henderson the Thirds and its Allie Stotzers and its Thayne Winslows. I could give you a Roman counterpart for every one of those"—he hesitates, then lets go with—"fuckers. And they all talked in the name of the Republic and the welfare of the plebs, the people, just the way your heroes do across the park."

Art listens intently. Despite his aversion to the upper class, to government interference with labor, despite the influence of a lifetime, he listens. Does Dennis Crawford really mean what he's saying?

"That's why we want men like you to help us," Crawford goes on. "We don't want to wreck your union— we want to help you protect it against the Ciceros and the kind of sweetheart deals Joey Hopper makes with George Henderson the Third. What they're doing isn't unionism, it's graft flying under the false colors of unionism."

Art is affected, but not convinced, especially when it comes to Joey Hopper. Okay, he never trusted George Henderson from the early days in Hendersonville. And he curses the day Mafiosos like Cicero brought their goons into the Brotherhood. But Joey has promised to weed them out.

"Joey Hopper and George Henderson are partners,"

Crawford says. "Joey Hopper and Vincent Cicero are
partners. I shouldn't tell you this because I suspect you'll
just go back and tell it to Joey. But we've come across
some very interesting documents in the possession of
Henderson's accountant, Henry Nettles. He was hiding in
a midwestern city in a third-rate hotel under a different
name. But we found him—before he destroyed his
records. Sal is staying up all night to study them. I'm not
giving away any secrets because George the Third already
knows what happened. I'll bet anything those lights
across the park mean that Joey is working Thayne Winslow and his staff overtime to sweat out some answers."

Art is unable to believe it. Sure, Joey plays rough.
He's always claimed you have to fight fire with fire, even
if that means using goons. And maybe he has been a little
soft on Henderson because George III helped him break
the open-shop, company-town setup that had tyrannized
Henderson County for more than half a century.

"Joey Hopper owns gas stations and taxicab companies and even some oil wells in the name of his wife
and Cicero's wife," Crawford says. "And the man who set
up the deals for him in return for preferential treatment
is George Henderson the Third."

"I still don't believe it," Art Nielsen says.

"Watch the next session of the hearings—when, by
the way, we hope you will testify voluntarily about your
paper-local troubles."

"I don't believe it," Art repeats. "Sure we may have
our crooks. Cicero, Lake, Mingus, J. B. Archer . . ."

"Oddly enough, we haven't found a single case so far
of Archer's being on the take from either management or

the mob," Crawford says. "It's just that he's become a slave—chained to Hopper's golden chariot."

"I don't believe it," Art says again. "I trust Joey. I'm gonna ask him myself face to face. This whole thing smells like a trick to get me to turn against 'im." He's on his feet now. "I'm getting out of here!"

Thoughtfully, Crawford watches him go. Santoro returns, along with Dave and Charley. Phil and other staff members are busy in the outer offices. There is no overtime on this job. Everybody is working around the clock.

"What you up to, Denny?" Sal asks. "Nielsen ran out of here like Tiny Lake was after him!"

"I took a calculated risk," Crawford explains. "If he's really this-way with Hopper, I told him a little too much. But I've been sizing him up. Art Nielsen is kind of the Hamlet of the IB. He honestly doesn't know whether to be or not to be. Still rank and file? Or personal assistant to a Joey Hopper he wants to believe in?"

Sal and Charley nod. Dave relights his dead cigar.

"The movies have it all wrong, Dave," Crawford smiles. "Vinnie One Eye smokes Turkish cigarettes through an elegant holder. And you chew on two-bit cigars like a poor man's Eddie G. Robinson."

"I'm really Bugsy Bender in disguise," Dave grins.

"Guess we're all getting a little punchy," Crawford says.

Charley nods. "So?"

"So let's work another hour."

39

*U*pset, but determined to find out for himself, Art hurries across the park to the gleaming glass and marble symbol of IBHT power, the national headquarters.

In the conference corner of Joey's paneled office he sees Lou Vass and a group of Thayne Winslow's lawyers "doing their homework" to counteract the Committee. The pressure is really on, Vass says. Subpoenas are falling like leaves in November. Joey Hopper? He flew up to Capital City. He and the Governor want to go through a lot of records up there before Crawford's raiders can get their hands on them.

Wild-eyed, Art thanks the harassed lawyer and runs out. Vass and his assistants shake their heads. With the new hearings about to start, everybody seems to be going up the wall.

Art hurries to his car and starts driving to Capital City. He is now of the privileged class allowed a new Buick every year from the IB motor pool. He races through the night, tires screaming, not slowing down until he jams on the brakes in Hopper's driveway. It is around three o'clock in the morning.

He keeps ringing the bell until Paula comes to the door in her night-robe. What in the world does Art want at this crazy hour? Joey? She has no idea where he is. She thought he was in Washington. No, Art says, they told him at headquarters that Joey had taken off for Capital City hours ago. Paula shrugs. Typical. These days Joey's more mysterious than ever. If it wasn't for her friend Monique, "The Late-Late Show," a friendly beer, and her darling Siamese cats, she'd wind up in the booby hatch.

Art looks at Paula and it saddens him—that marvelous, lithe, high-spirited cheerleader, the happy-eyed kid he was crazy about once upon a time in Hendersonville. Now her figure is gone—she's on her way to being sloppy fat—and her hair, everything about her, shows she has let herself go. The only time she dolls herself up is when Joey needs her for the loyal-wife act at public functions.

She invites Art into her bedroom, where she is watching "The Late-Late Show." Half a dozen cats are sprawled on her bed now. One thing she is an expert on, she says, is old movies. She may be the only person in America who has seen every Ronald Reagan feature! Once Joey got to be the Great White Father of the IB, you'd think at least we'd have a big house in Georgetown or one of those big country estates in Virginia. But not Joey. Now he lives in that hotel in Washington and she slowly goes nuts in this crummy twenty-five-thousand-dollar dump he refuses to sell. "You should see Vinnie

Cicero's home," she says. "It's like a Roman palace. The
swimming pool alone is twice as long as this house and it's
got colored lights under the water. Monique has me out
there for lunch a lot and I just about turn green with
envy."

"But that's what still gets me about Joey," Art is
grasping at the last straw of loyalty. "I've been in
the homes of lots of our vice-presidents. They look like
movie-star castles. But Joey, somehow he still manages to
stay simple. Same ready-made clothes. And even though
it's tough on you, there is something nice about the way
he hangs on to the same house he bought when he made
the move from Hendersonville."

"Nice my eye," Paula says. "Oh, I could tell you
some things. Things that would make you wish you was
dead. The way I feel a good half the time."

"Like what, Paula?" Art begs. "You and me, we're
like brother and sister—you c'n tell me."

Paula refills her glass. "Like the way he keeps
stickin' things in front of my face," she goes on. "Sign this
. . . sign that—I don't even know what the hell I'm
signin'—all of a sudden it turns out I'm the president of a
chain of gas stations called Agerts, it's like my maiden
name spelled backwards. If you ask me, the whole thing
is backwards and upside down. Don't laugh."

"Who's laughing?"

"And then there's a taxicab company in Omaha, I
even forget the name of it, but me an' Monique, we're
supposed t' be the owners. We even have a racing stable
called the P&M—don't ask me how! All I know is some
sonofabitch from the Senate Committee comes to ask me

about 'em. He probably thought I was a dirty liar, but I
didn't even know Monique and I owned the damned
things. A hundred 'n' eighty-five thousand bucks we
made in the last two years, this snoop from Washington
tries to tell me. Oh yeah? Where is it? Joey doesn't even
keep a bank account. I don't understand him, Art. It's an
awful thing lying in bed next to a man you're scared to
death of. If I wasn't raised old-fashioned Catholic from
the old country, I swear t' God I'd divorce him. Only I'd
be scared to. That's the whole trouble, Art. Everybody in
the union is scared of him. You're scared of him. Governor Winslow is scared of him. J. B. Archer is scared of
him. Oh, to hell with it," she suddenly decides. "Let's you
and me just sit up all night and get stinkin'—"

Art makes his apologies. He'd like to stay and keep
her company. But he drove out from Washington for a
specific purpose. He's got to see it through.

"Okay," she gives in. "If you see the Almighty President of the International Brotherhood, tell him the President of Agerts Oil Company and apparently numerous
other enterprises misses her husband like holy hell."

Left to her cats, her beer, and her well-thumbed *True
Romances*, she turns back to Dale Robertson in *Son of
Sinbad*.

Art Nielsen hurries off to the Sherwood Hills mansion of J. B. Archer. Although it is now only an hour or so
before dawn, the lights are still on. In his monogrammed
silk robe, J.B. explains that he and his wife, Helen, have
been talking all night, after receiving a subpoena to ap-

pear before the next session of hearings into the "improper activities" of the IBHT.

"That's what I come to see you about," Art says. His mind is crackling with doubts and confusion. Can Joey actually be partners with Vinnie Cicero? Is that how Cicero got his phony jukebox charters so easily and why Joey never raised a finger to protect the integrity of the locals he and Art started together? He couldn't quite bring himself to believe it from Dennis Crawford and his staff. But when he got the word direct from Paula—without her quite realizing what she was saying—it made him sick to his stomach. And the crazy part is, all the time he thought it was J.B. taking tips and selling out to the bosses.

"I never took a tip in my life," J.B. says. "It may look it from the way I live, but I never took a dime to soften a contract. And I think the Ciceros are the curse of the labor movement, same as you do. Don't you think I know this is no way to run a trade union?"

"Listen, J.B. Let me put it to you straight. If you know all this—why don't you quit?"

Archer pours himself another strong shot of Chivas Regal. "That's a good question, Art. At the Convention, and for as long afterward as I could make myself believe it, I honestly thought Joey might be able to use the Ciceros to assure the election and get into some big cities, like Chicago, where we were hitting stone walls—and then eventually throw the bums out. I kept hoping, that's the God's truth, I kept hoping and maybe I was fool enough or vain enough to think Joey would listen to me."

"But no dice?"

"Right now I'd say it would be hard to peg where Joey Hopper ends and the mob begins. I don't know who owns who, they own each other. They're into everything, not just coin machines but garbage collection, taxicabs, insurance—Art, it nearly kills me to say it but it's just about as bad as Denny Boy and his bloodhounds are trying to make out."

"Then why don't you quit?" Art asks again, asking himself the same question.

J.B. looks around. "Doesn't this place tell the story? And the new Caddy in the garage? And the free vacations in Miami or Honolulu or Puerto Rico every winter? And don't forget the pension—that's where he's got us by the balls—no International in the country can touch our pensions—a truck driver with thirty years' service can live out his days in Florida on fifteen thousand a year. If I can stick it out six more years, I'll retire on fifty thousand— and fringes. I may live in a gutter, Art, but it's a golden gutter."

"You could also end up with a hole in your head," Art says, rubbing a scar from his elevator trip.

"Always possible," J.B. agrees. "The dinosaurs know I hate their guts just like—excuse me—just *as* they hate mine. But we have one thing in common—and it's a pretty big thing, maybe the biggest thing in the whole country—your friend and mine, Joey Hopper."

"What are you going to tell the Committee?" Art asks.

"I'll talk to them," J.B. says. "I won't tell them anything, but I'll answer young Mr. Crawford's questions very fully, if you know what I mean. I'll point out our trade-union accomplishments—and believe me, we've got them. I'll wrack my mind to handle the hard ones. I won't exactly lie, I just won't exactly tell the truth."

"But how can you live with it?" Art asks. "That's what's driving me nuts. How do you live with it, at the end of the road?"

"You know what Harry Truman said, Art: 'If you can't stand the heat, stay out of the kitchen.' I only go into the kitchen when I have to—and I hold my nose. Meanwhile I do the best I can for the men. Our overall hourly rate is high. Our benefits are nearly as sweet as Dubinsky got for his garment workers. Except in the racket locals where the mob sells out our boys, they do all right. Sure, the goniffs take it in fistfuls—how can you help it when fifty million is coming in every month? I sleep nights by telling myself I'm doing as honest a trade-union job as I can, considering I'm surrounded by dinosaurs."

"Make me a drink," Art says. "Tonight Paula was telling me her world is upside down. Mine is like a barrel going over Niagara. Joey, who—well, frankly, I idolized him—it's like you're swimming in a beautiful clear lake and all of a sudden it turns out to be a cesspool. You—like I said—I put you down for a labor crook the minute I met you. I may not admire you now but at least for the first time I think I understand you. And Dennis Crawford, when he first took after the IBHT, I hated his guts—a rich, smart-aleck, antilabor kid on the make. Now I'm be-

ginning to believe that he isn't trying to break our union
—he's just trying to break the racketeer hold that Joey has
let Vinnie One Eye and the rest of them box us in with.
Maybe I'm not making sense, I'm half lit, I'm worn out,
but . . ."

"You're making sense," J.B. says gently. "You're just
starting to go through now what I did a long time ago. I
learned to live with it. You haven't."

"I don't want to! You can have your big house and
your new Caddy and your fancy egghead self-justification
about how much you're doing for the rank and file—except here and there where honest working stiffs get their
brains knocked out just for standing up at a meeting and
asking for their rights."

"Art, I couldn't agree with you more," J.B. says. "But
I've only got six more years to hang on. So if you were to
quote me on what I've been telling you tonight, I'd have
to call you a liar. I've got to go down the line for J for
Justice, T for Tough, H for the Hook he holds me on—
Hopper."

"Thanks for the drink." Art's hand is shaking as he
puts down his glass. "I wish you had never bought us that
first one in Hendersonville."

Awash in his golden gutter, J.B. shrugs and pours
himself another. "Be careful, Art," he says, and means it.
"Stay out of elevators."

*B*y the time Art Nielsen reaches his comfortable home in Reston, it is already daylight—around seven in the morning. Edna, in her bathrobe, greets him hysterically. She is just getting ready to feed the children. When he didn't come home, she was frantic—she thought that even with the protection of his headquarters job the Cicero crowd had gotten to him again. He apologizes—he's had mixed feelings about the IB ever since the crunch in Hendersonville. But the things he's heard from Dennis Crawford—he just had to try and check out for himself.

"So you drove all the way to Cap City to get the lowdown from Paula? I called her at four o'clock this morning when you still weren't home."

"Eddie," he says, "we're packing up. We're getting out. It's a nice house, all paid for by the union, and we've got a Caddy, ditto, but we're getting out. I don't want to be another J. B. Archer—that's where I'm headed. A vice-president in ten years, maybe, with an unlimited expense account—and my balls in Joey's wringer."

Edna stares at him. "Out of the IB?"

"Out," Art says. "I came down to Washington to help clean things up. It's like trying to clean out a sewer. The more scrubbing you do, the more shit pours through and you climb out twice as filthy as you went in."

"But what'll we do—how will we live?"

"We'll go home. Hendersonville. We've got a little money put away. And I could get a small loan from the bank maybe. Open a motel, okay?—be our own boss."

"But unions have been our whole life, Art, and your old man's. You and me, Paula and Joey, instead of lovers' lanes we did our courting on the picket lines. How can you walk away?"

"Eddie, I'd never walk away from my union—if it was legit. Remember that Statement of Policy Joey ran on? J.B.'s beautiful Ten Commandments of Labor Democracy? Joey's broken every one of 'em—no wonder the AFL-CIO voted us out. We're not a labor union any more, Ed, that's why I've got to get out—we're an International Brotherhood of Crooks and Racketeers, with a million and a half members too bullshitted or scared to stand up and be counted."

Edna puts her arms around him. "Now you listen to me, honey: I love Reston, it's swell for the kids. I was looking to the time when we'd saved enough to put 'em through college and retire on maybe thirty thousand a year. . . ."

"That's the trouble," Art says. "The union—in Pop's time it was the real thing. Now everybody's looking for the second car and the second television set and the condominium in Florida. And if the Joey Hoppers make deals with crooked bosses and with hoods, who cares, who really cares? As long as we're comfortable? And live happily ever after?"

"You're all upset," Edna says, serving him coffee.

"You've been listening to do-gooders like Dennis Crawford. . . ."

"I've been listening to Paula. She's a mess, Eddie. I
hate to say it but that's what she is. She used to be a
good, honest, hardworking girl—and now she owns companies that have sweetheart contracts with her husband's
own union—he's making a fortune, Eddie. . . ."

"God knows what he does with it—you sure don't see
it on him," Edna says.

"I know. It's a mystery," Art admits. "Paula doesn't
understand it. He must have it buried in the ground
somewhere."

"Like some kind of a miser."

"Only what he likes to take out and run through his
hands in the middle of the night isn't money—it's power."

The phone rings. Edna answers it. "It's Joey," she
says. "He wants to see you at the office right away."

He slowly sets down his cup. Edna hugs him. "Art,
be careful. Whatever you do, be careful."

"Don't worry," he says. "I'm not the hero type."

41

Art finds Joey in his private gymnasium at IB headquarters. With its sophisticated equipment—including a
sauna and Jacuzzi—it's a long way from the improvised

workout room in Capital City. Joey, in an IBHT sweat
suit, is hurling a medicine ball back and forth with his
trainer, a onetime heavyweight contender. All these
years, while the men around him have grown softer and
flabbier, Joey has managed to stay in Muscle Hollow
shape, his belly hard and tight, still able to take a solid
punch in the gut.

"Be with you in a minute, Art," Joey says, showing
no sign of tension or animosity as he fires the ball back
hard at his trainer. "You should come in and use this gym
half an hour every day. I'm thinking of making it a must
for all my officers. Shit, if Denny Boy plays squash all
winter, we better shape up, too." Again he catches the
heavy leather ball against his stomach and hurls it back
just as hard.

"This is the only fella I know c'n wear me out," the
old heavyweight grins.

The telephone rings. Joey doesn't let his workouts interfere with running the IBHT. There are phones in the
gym, in the sauna, even in the shower room. Joey Hopper
is never out of touch.

"It's Mr. Bailey, in New York," the trainer says.

Sweating healthily, Joey grabs the phone, "Hello,
Handsome, how are all the ships at sea?—listen, be down
here at three on the dot tomorrow. I'll have Jackson in
from the West Coast and Aparacio from San Juan. Better
figure to stay overnight. There'll be a lot to do. Right.
Stop worryin' about Jackson bein' a Commie. This is too
big for that kind of shit. Let Hopper do the worryin' for
ya. My friend, I promise, ya won't get hurt. Hopper looks
after his own. Check. Three on the nose. Okay, Handsome."

He hangs up, pleased with himself. He strips, with just a towel around his middle, and stretches out on the rubbing table. As the trainer works over his muscles, Joey talks to Art rapid-fire. This job gets more exciting every day. So those AFL-CIO jerk-offs think they can hurt his feelings by thumbing him out of their crummy organization? Has he got news for them!

"Turn over," the trainer says.

Joey does, but doesn't stop talking. He's putting together a joint organization of *all* transportation workers, tying in the longshoremen from the East Coast with the longshoremen on the West Coast—screw their political differences. He's tying in the sailors of the Atlantic, the Pacific, and the Gulf. He's tying in everything that moves by land, sea, or air—from Puerto Rico to Honolulu!

He sits up on the table and takes a quick phone call from San Francisco. "Fine, Larry, don't worry about Bailey—all you gotta do is trust Hopper—I'll have a car meet you at the airport—three on the button."

He hangs up. "Then, when we've got truckers, sailors, and the longshore, we'll go after the airlines. One big union of transportation. As an old union man, it should warm your heart, Art. One Big Union, just the way the Wobblies used to dream it around the hobo fires."

Joey's exuberance is balanced by Art's silence. Joey gets off the table. "What's the matter with you, Art? What's buggin' you? Why'd you go see Paula in the middle of the night?"

"Joey—I want my withdrawal card from the IBHT."

Joey waits and thinks. "Art, I sent you into that

Committee to help keep them from breakin' us up. You know why they hate us—? 'Cause we're the fastest-growin' union in America. You haven't let that Ivy League headline-hunter, an asshole who never met a payroll or worked for bread a fuckin' day in his life—you aren't lettin' him sell you a bill of goods, are ya, Art?"

"Joey, nobody's sold me a bill of goods. But nobody. All I'm asking for is my withdrawal card. I want to resign from the IB. I don't want to spy for you or the Committee. I don't want to fink to the Committee on you. You and Crawford can fight it out between yourselves. I just don't want to get caught in the middle."

"Art, I'm disappointed in you. I thought you'd have more imagination."

"J. B. Archer has enough imagination for the two of us. I don't want to be a power like you, or a mind—I mean, a whore—like him."

"Look, I don't have time for long-winded explanations," Joey says. "You want to be alone—better be sure you stay alone. Don't get too chummy with antilabor glamour boys who want to climb over the truck driver's back into the Senate. I think you know what I mean."

"Antilabor? Nobody calls me antilabor, Joey, not even the great President Hopper. I'm as prolabor as the day we organized Local Number One—ya called it 101, because you was thinking of a hundred behind it and a thousand to come after it. You were thinking of millions, and I was thinking of the guys who trusted us to do a job for them."

"I'm still doing a job for them, on a level you can't even conceive of," Joey says.

"And letting the hoods and the sweethearts steal 'em blind?"

"Go home, Art," Joey says. "You belong back in Hendersonville. You're small-town, boy."

"I heard J. B. Archer say that to me once," Art answers. "Poor J.B."

"Poor J.B. will retire with a pension of fifty thousand dollars a year for life," Joey says.

"If he keeps his nose clean," Art says.

"He'll keep his nose clean," Joey says. "So will you."

"Is that a threat, Joey?"

"Of course that's not a threat, Art." Joey taps Art good-naturedly on the chin. "I'm not a brass-knuckle boy like—"

"Like Tiny Lake?"

"I'm sorry about Tiny. It's a tough world and sometimes we need tough hands to run it. Anyway, good luck back home. All my love to Edna. Have to hurry and get dressed now. Big meeting in three hours. And it's five hundred miles away."

"George Henderson's private plane should get you there in time," Art says, and limps away.

"Fuckin' ingrate," Joey says as he watches Art walk out on him. "Wasn't for me, that bum would still be pushing an oil rig for Henderson & Son!"

"I got the shower runnin', boss," the old fighter says.

"Thanks, slugger. Be sure ya get me out in time to make that plane." Joey steps into the shower, turning the water on even harder, enjoying the sting.

George Henderson III has been hiding out in his rustic hunting lodge that can be reached only by seaplane. Joey Hopper flies in with Winslow and Vass to meet him.

No longer the new-look tycoon who was going to show his father how to use sweetheart contracts to destroy competitors, the younger Henderson has aged in a hurry. When Joey knocks on the heavy, bolted door, George has his butler ask who it is. Every knock may be a process server.

"It's Joey Hopper, goddammit! Open the goddam door, George," Joey orders.

Inside, in front of the roaring fire, George confides his fears. He has destroyed some of his correspondence with Joey, but unfortunately his father has proved very difficult. He has insisted on satisfying the Committee's demands for the company records. And once Henry Nettles was located—

"You should've had him get sick and die if you had to," Joey breaks in. "An old queen like Nettles don't have the guts to do anything but tell the truth."

"You mean, I should have had him killed?"

"I never say *kill*," Joey reminds him. "But what was that crap you were giving me when we made our first deal—something about a kraut egghead?"

"Nietzsche?"

"Yeah, that's the bum. The basic drive in every man is the will to power."

"You have quite a memory," George says almost regretfully.

"Except when he's before the Committee," Lou Vass adds dryly.

"When I want comedians, I'll hire Bob Hope," Joey snaps.

George pours himself a cognac. "Look, Joey, I want you to understand. I believe in Nietzsche as a philosophy, but—"

"When it comes to putting it into practice, you choke," Joey cuts him off.

"Possibly," George admits. "Henderson & Son is a traditional, long-established firm. I can't hide the fact that I dread having to explain to the Committee some of those documents that have unfortunately fallen into their hands."

"Explain nothin'! If you can't talk around their fuckin' questions"—Joey turns to Winslow—"whatta ya call it, Guv, filibuster 'em?—then take the Fifth. Maybe your rich friends at the country club will cut you dead, but at least they can't put you in jail."

"I'm not so sure—there is a law called commercial bribery. I actually could go to jail, Joey. That's why I've decided—I think it would be better for all of us if I took a long trip to Europe until this thing blows over."

"You will like hell, George," Joey says. "Ya run out on the subpoena and it's like admittin' ya guilty. That's what Honest Bill Reed tried to do and when they got 'im back he was shakin' like a bowl o' Jell-O. All you had to do was look at 'im an' ya knew his days of taking palsie-walsie pictures with the Prez at the White House was all over. Stand your ground, goddammit! Fight back! Sure Crawford is gettin' tough. So we gotta get tougher. Hell, we've got to have better lawyers than they've got, we pay 'em more—don't we, Thayne? George, if ya try t' sneak out on me I'll break ya goddam Nietchee book over ya goddam head. Tough it out! When ya gimme the gas-station deal that night at the Broadmore you was startin' t' go f' the big chips. If ya gonna play with the big boys, walk taller!"

Winslow has been trying to get a word in but Joey tells him to shut up. And the once-proud Governor has to eat it. Lou Vass is very quiet. He cannot quite hide his distaste for Joey's methods.

The butler enters. "Dinner is served, sir."

"I ain't stayin' f'r the chow." Joey rises. "I'll grab a sandwich on the plane. I got these maritime guys comin' in from the East Coast and the West Coast: Vinnie Cicero's pals from the New York waterfront and Larry's Commie bastards from San Fran. I wanna get this one big transportation union all signed 'n' delivered before Denny Boy and his Girl Scouts start throwin' their new shit at me. . . ."

He strides toward the door. "Tell ya pilot let's get the kite in the air."

He gestures rudely toward Winslow. "Thayne, I

want you with me. Vass, you stay with George and read
'im some Nietchee f' a bedtime story. Try t' teach 'im how
to answer them questions so he c'n sound like the honorable president of that long-established institution, Henderson & Son, and still not tell 'em a fuckin' thing."

Out slams Joey Hopper. George Henderson the
Third sinks deeper into the great leather couch facing the
roaring fire.

*I*n Dennis Crawford's suite in the Old Senate Office
Building, the work load and the tempo are mounting.
The charts on the wall are more detailed, the files are fat-
ter, the staff—headed by Dave, Phil, Charley, and
Sal—has been doubled.

Crawford, in his shirt sleeves with tie pulled down,
tousled hair over his forehead, is questioning a small,
harassed coin-machine businessman:

"Mr. Lewis, you consider yourself a legitimate jukebox operator, isn't that true? And our investigators have
learned that two of Vincent Cicero's boys came into a location where you had a box and beat you so badly your

doctor says your health has been permanently impaired, isn't that true?"

Sam Lewis is another frightened, broken, little man. "That's true, Mr. Crawford, sir."

"And as a result of the beating you agreed to take Cicero in as a full partner—thereby cutting your annual income from sixty thousand dollars a year to thirty, right?"

"I'm afraid that's right, Mr. Crawford."

"And yet, if I were to ask you at the hearings to give me the same honest answer you're giving me here and to identify the two hoodlums who beat you almost to death, on the pretext that they were 'union' and you were 'anti-union,' what would you say?"

Lewis lowers his face to his hands and starts to sob. "I don't know, Mr. Crawford. I don't know what I'd say. I'm not a strong man, Mr. Crawford. I'm on a pacemaker. I just wish you wouldn't make me say the names in public, Mr. Crawford."

Crawford sighs. More of the same. "Okay, Mr. Lewis. Thanks for coming in. I don't think we'll call you."

Sam Lewis weeps his gratitude and shuffles out.

For a moment Crawford gives in to weakness and drops his head on his desk. Dave Edelman comes over. His head still on the desk, Crawford asks, "How we doing, Dave?"

"I've been talking to Bugsy Bender, trying to scare him into talking, but he's got his orders."

"That's the trouble," Crawford says, sitting up. "The Bugsy Benders and the Three Fingers Joneses—nobody expects them to talk. But when you come up against legitimate small businessmen like Mr. Lewis, who just left in tears—might as well kill his subpoena, he'll lie or take the Fifth, protect the mobster who cut himself in. Who's running this country, Dave, the people or the Ciceros? And Cicero's bosses?"

"I'm still betting on the people," Dave says, filling the air with more cigar smoke.

Crawford shrugs. "I don't know. Ever since you blocked that Cornell punt and fell on it for a Columbia touchdown, you've been an impossible optimist. Sam Lewis is people. The drivers, the IB members who get their treasury looted and are scared to speak up, they're people. Maybe it's something wrong with the people, Dave. Maybe they just don't care enough."

Dave says, "Denny, you left the office at two this morning and got back here at eight. That's just tiredness talking. Sooner or later we've got to win."

The simple optimism strikes both Crawford's humor and his combativeness. "Roar, lion, roar!" he says. Then, all business again: "How's Sal doing?"

"Terrific," Dave says. "He's chopping the Henderson bank statements into little pieces."

"Good, only all that paper stuff needs flesh and blood to back it up. And George Henderson the Third, we can't even find him. A great lion of industry running like a scared rabbit."

"Don't worry, we'll find him. In spite of that TV series, I've still got faith in the FBI."

Crawford laughs. "Are you always this funny, Dave? Or am I just so tired I'll laugh at anything?" Before Dave

can quip again, he has an idea. "What about Art Nielsen?"

"No answer at his house. All closed up. The word is
he's pulled out of the organization."

"And he didn't come in to say good-bye to us, either?" Crawford muses. "Dave, he could be important.
We've got checks, we've got records, we've got conflict-
of-interest contracts on Joey Hopper and tie-ins with his
wife and Cicero's, even if the poor girls didn't know it—
but what we need is a live witness from the inside. Art
Nielsen would be a natural. Let's go talk to him, Dave.
See if we can fly up tonight."

"There's an eleven o'clock to Capital City," Dave
says. "We can air-taxi from there in about thirty minutes. . . ."

Sal Santoro runs in with a file, happy over his thick
glasses. "Some of these memos from George Henderson to
Joey Hopper are beautiful," he says. "He even quotes
Nietzsche as the reason for forming the Agerts Oil Company."

"Good work, Sal." Crawford is sorting documents,
getting ready to go. "If we don't succeed in finding Henderson, let's be sure and get out a subpoena for
Nietzsche, F. W., address unknown. . . ."

Jan Crawford hurries in, with a small overnight case.
He reacts guiltily. "Darling, I was just about to call you,
to say I wouldn't be home tonight. I'll be back in time for
breakfast."

"I know it. I packed your overnight bag."

"I don't understand it."

"ESP."

"I spell it L-O-V-E," he says, taking the small bag and hugging her.

"I like the lyric, Chief," Dave Edelman comments without removing his cigar. "With the right tune it could be a hit."

"Leave him alone," Jan says. "As the author of three rejected short stories, he knows how tough it is to write about love. Anyway, I didn't marry Shakespeare. I married the Rackets Committee."

The Crawfords walk out, arms around each other, Dave Edelman following them in a cloud of cigar smoke.

Dave calls across to Phil Mahoney, working with a witness at his desk on the other side of the room. "Phil, will you please call Rose and tell her"—he pauses—"tell her if we ever nail Joey Hopper I'd like to marry her again—even if I trip on my long white beard on the way to the altar."

Phil Mahoney nods over his slender-stemmed pipe and suppresses a smile as his colleagues exit.

44

Later that night a small plane sets Crawford and Edelman down on the Hendersonville airstrip. As a cab takes them to Nielsen's house, they are followed at a discreet distance by a black Cadillac with Tiny Lake at the wheel, backed by Three Fingers, Bugsy Bender, and Champ Christoli.

Art Nielsen and his family take a dim view of the emissaries from the Committee. They spell trouble and that's exactly what Art has quit the IBHT to avoid. Especially now that Edna is expecting their third child.

Crawford speaks more passionately than he ever has before:

"Art, what you're involved in seems to be the creeping sickness of the country. Corruption—it's a cancer. And it's been spreading like crazy in the last twenty years."

Art doesn't disagree but wishes Crawford would go away.

"That's the enemy, Art. Corruption creeping into everything, from nursing homes to defense contracts to labor. It's a lot bigger than Henderson and Cicero and the jukebox boyos you've run up against. If you think of a thousand Hendersons and a thousand Ciceros all around the country, you begin to get the picture. And get one thing straight, Art. This isn't a fight against the labor movement. We see ourselves *helping* the movement, which means waking up the whole country to an alliance that involves some giant corporations, godfathers, and friends in high places, right up to the White House. Damned near an underground government!"

He pauses, realizing he's let his own convictions run away with him, overwhelming the Nielsens. "If that sounds heavy, I'm sorry, but that's the story, and you better believe it."

"But what can Art do about it?" Edna asks. "What can one man do?"

Dave fields this one. "Maybe a lot more than you think, Mrs. Nielsen. We've worked like hell to get ready for the hearings, to show that a couple of hundred IB officials are getting rich on your sweat and blood. But it's only words—even if it's ten million words—unless the honest members—and there's a hell of a lot of you—back us up. In public. Under oath."

"Art, you're a perfect example," Crawford picks up. "If just a few men like you will get up and tell the people what you've gone through, maybe it could start the ball rolling. And maybe you could get rid of the mobsters who have a headlock on your union. What I'm asking you to do is testify, Art. Hell, I'm begging you!"

There is an awkward silence. "If I could only believe it'd do any good . . ." Art mutters.

"I hope you won't take this wrong, Mr. Crawford," Edna finally says. "What you say about the IB—I guess it's pretty true. And we're sick about what's happened to Art, and lots of others. But it's easy for you to sit there and tell us what to do. You aren't in any danger. The black Cadillacs don't follow you around. They don't crowd you into elevators and leave you choking in your own blood. You've got nothing to lose."

Dave Edelman lights his cigar. "I want to tell you folks something. I know Dennis would never mention it. When this investigation started two years ago, there was a lot of talk about his running for the Senate. But the power-brokers came and warned him, don't go too hard on Bill Reed, he's got a lot of political clout—and now they're saying the same thing about Joey Hopper. With Thayne Winslow, and the IBHT millions, and the political action committee that J. B. Archer has set up for him, Hopper can throw enough weight around to make Dennis a liability. Why start with a candidate who's already got a million enemies? And don't forget the Syndicate money against him. Hundred-dollar bills flying around like snowflakes."

Crawford nods. "I admit it, Art," he says wryly. "I wouldn't mind being a Senator. But I can promise you this: I'm not going to make a single compromise to get there. Some of our Committee are afraid we'll antagonize management if we push Henderson and other white-collar crooks too far—and that we'll alienate labor if we try to put Joey Hopper and other racketeers in jail. Maybe—but I'm going to push this investigation all the way, Art. Sure, I happen to have money, and they won't brass-knuckle me, at least not physically. Though there's always a danger that—"

He catches himself. "Well, we've taken up enough of your time. Think about it, Art. I'll call you again in a few days. Things are moving fast. What we dug up on Bill Reed was bad enough. What we're digging up now is a hundred times worse."

"But Joey Hopper is a hundred times tougher," Art says.

Crawford and Dave are at the door. "Thanks for hearing us out. And thanks for the coffee, Mrs. Nielsen. See you, Art."

As the investigators get into their cab and drive off, Art looks down the street. Slowly a black Cadillac moves forward and parks in front of the house. Then another, and another.

Art shuts the door and latches it. "Looks like a parking lot out there," he says, as he goes to the hall closet, gets out his shotgun, and loads it.

Edna goes into his arms, terrified. "Oh, God, why doesn't Crawford leave us alone? Let *him* save the country!"

Art stares at his shotgun. "I never thought of using this on anything bigger than ducks. . . ."

He peers out through the side curtains. The black Cadillacs are waiting like giant buzzards.

Later that night: Edna has fallen asleep. Art is pacing. He looks out the bedroom window. The buzzards are still there. The phone rings. Art isn't going to answer it. But when it keeps ringing, Edna reaches for it sleepily.

"My name is Ruby," the caller says. "I just want you to know that I'm going to have a kid in two months and that cunt-hound you're married to is who knocked me up. If he don't come over an' help me with money right away, I'm gonna take him to court."

The woman hangs up. Edna asks Art, "You know a girl named Ruby?"

"Who?"

"She says she's going to have your baby."

Art shakes his head. "That's an old one. The only kid

I can take any credit for is right here." He taps her stomach gently and kisses her. "Don't answer the phone any more."

"And you didn't even say *yes* to Crawford." Edna is near tears. "Imagine what would happen if . . ."

The phone starts ringing again. They ignore it but it wakes the baby, Florrie, and she starts to whimper. Edna goes to her. "This world is so mean, sometimes I wish you didn't have to grow up."

The phone keeps ringing.

Beverly Lambert's bedroom has a king-size bed, a soft red glow, and a Scott stereo that is playing a haunting Stan Getz improvisation. The animal sounds of lovemaking mount to a climax. Beverly, naked under the silken sheets, studies Joey Hopper as he gets out of bed and pulls up his trousers.

"What time is it?" he asks, putting on his shoes.

Beverly parodies a telephone time signal. "When you hear the to-an it will be exactly tey-en-seventeen. This is a prerecorded announcement." She sits up, holding the blue silk sheets to her breast. "Even with that big cock you're a lousy lover. At least J.B. used to take off his clothes and stay all night. And we used to talk, for Christ sake—before, during, and after."

"That's why he'll never move higher than third vice-president," Joey says, quickly finishing dressing. "I gotta catch a plane out to Hendersonville. Keep the office fires burning."

"Sometimes I wish one of those planes would crash," she says, reaching for a cigarette as Joey hurries to the door. "But if I know you, you'd be the only one to get up and walk away."

45

Now it is Joey Hopper's turn to lead his fleet of black Cadillacs to Art Nielsen's door. Tiny Lake is with him, and Three Fingers, and in the rear the other juke-"unionists," Champ, Bugsy, and Harry the Horse. Also some of the knee-breakers from the early Capital City days, Ned Green, Ace Huddicker . . .

Cocky as ever, Joey gets out and tells them to wait. This shouldn't take long.

Joey enters the Nielsen home with his usual exuberance. He has come because he remembered it was young Joey's third birthday. He's brought some presents for the kids: boxing gloves for Joey—"Let 'im learn to keep his left up early," he laughs—and a large, beautiful doll for Florrie. He asks Edna how she's feeling—Paula is

fine and sends love—they all have to get together soon—
maybe for the christening of the Nielsens' third child!

Art Nielsen has been drinking, something he never
did before. His nerves are cracking.

Joey orders everybody out—Edna, the old father,
young Tommy, grown into a man now, a fact that Joey
acknowledges with a sturdy slap on the shoulder. "I hear
ya a full-fledged member of 101—boy, how things
change!"

"They sure do," Tommy says noncommittally.

"Okay, beat it," Joey thumbs, used to giving orders.
Of Tommy, he says, "Pretty strong kid, huh? But he ain't
got the old charm like Pinky."

"Tommy's a good kid," Art says. "A lot of the old-
timers, like Deac and Porky, think he's got the makings of
a real take-over guy. The way you used to be."

Joey flares. "Don't give me that use-t'-be crap, Art.
Hopper has done more for the workin' man than any
other sonuvabitch in these whole United States. You been
listenin' to too much of that union-bustin' shinola from
Denny Boy."

"*Hopper*," Art says. "You and I peddled papers together when we were ten. You don't have to call yourself
Hopper with me."

"Art, you're right," Joey agrees. "I'm sorry. I deal
with so many people all day, and I wanna make 'em
know who's talkin'—it gets to be a habit."

He gestures toward Art's bottle of Four Roses.
"Okay, pour us both a shot. Old friends oughta drink together." They touch glasses. "What I come to say is—I
know Denny's been up here talkin' t' ya—"

"You've had your boys watching and calling my house all night—I'm afraid Edna's gonna have a miscarriage," Art says.

"I'm sorry," Joey says. "Believe me, I don't want to give you a bad time. Hopper—I mean *I* haven't forgotten what you and I did together t' knock the open shop outa the box here, Art. I've flown up to talk t' ya because I don't want t' see you fall into no antiunion trap—I don't want to see you get hurt, Art. I want ya t' give me ya word for old times' sake not to testify against us."

Art takes another drink. "Crawford wants me t' give 'im my word—you want me to give you my word—and me, I just want to live my life. Is that too much to ask?"

"With the hearings about to open, frankly yes," Joey says. "You sit tight and take the Fifth if they call you and you're set with a pension for life. You think Denny Crawford worries one good goddam about you? You think he gives a fuck about your kids, how you 'n' Edna are gonna live . . . ?"

Art stands up, staggering. "Joey, shut up. Stop crowding me. My head feels like it's splittin' open—like a watermelon. If you want to know the truth, I wish I was dead. I wish I was on an island somewhere catching fish and eating coconuts. I'm going nuts. Just leave me alone 'n' get out of here. . . ."

Joey's eyes turn inward. "You mean you're throwing me out, Art?"

"Get out, goddammit, get out," Art shouts, staggering, half drunk, half hysterical. "I wanna go to Tahiti or the North Pole, anyplace where they don't have Cadillacs and payoffs and jukeboxes with phony-union labels. . . ."

Hardly knowing what he is doing, Art pushes Joey out the door.

"What took so long?" Tiny asks.

Joey shakes his head. "I'm afraid Denny Boy has scrambled his brains. If they call him as a witness, he's liable to say anything."

"So we may have to discourage him a little more?" Tiny asks.

Joey gets into the Cadillac and it speeds off. "I figured I could straighten him out, but . . ."

"But he's gonna need a stronger dose?"

Joey leans back and closes his eyes.

An Italian luxury liner is sailing in half an hour. At the dock George Henderson III and his aloof wife, Ashley, hurry out of a cab and tell the porter to take their bags to the third-class gangplank. George wears an English hat with the brim pulled down over his eyes. Ashley is without furs. Their baggage is inconspicuous.

As they hurry into the pier, George mutters to the disgruntled Ashley not to worry; as soon as they are beyond the twelve-mile limit, he has made arrangements for them to be moved up to a deluxe first-class suite. But the third-class gangplank should fool the slow-witted FBI.

They make it successfully onto the ship and to their inside cabin on Deck D. George III is encouraged. Things are working out fine. The power principle, the dynamics of the superman win out again over the proles.

But once inside their tiny state-room, there is a knock on the door, and Dave Edelman and Charley Walker enter with a subpoena for the new hearings.

George Henderson is all courtesy. May he just have a moment to collect his things, some of which he has already distributed in the head?

He exits into the bathroom. There is a long pause while Dave and Charley wait with Ashley. Then they hear a groan—and a heavy fall. They throw open the bathroom door. On the shaving mirror is written in blood: "The thought of suicide is a great consolation"—Nietz . . .

Ashley manages to produce the appropriate responses. "Please help keep the press away from me. I loved my husband very much. He has been very depressed lately. All this harassment . . ."

Frustrated, Dave and Charley nod at each other as they turn away.

Now the hearings begin again, digested through a Chancellor-Brinkley Report which Art Nielsen and his family are watching on their TV set.

David Brinkley is saying, "Well, one of this country's best-known labor leaders—even though the AFL-CIO has

*made it clear it wants no part of him—Vice-President of
the IBHT Vincent 'One Eye' Cicero, was asked some
questions today by Dennis Crawford, chief counsel of the
Senate Committee on Improper Activities in Labor or
Management. Mr. Cicero wore a white Sulka tie and a
fine Italian suit. His clothes, while in good taste as always, spoke louder than his words. . . ."*

"Mr. Cicero, are you president of Local 333 of the International Brotherhood of Haulers and Truckers and
Auxiliary Workers?"

"I decline to answer on the grounds . . ."

"Mr. Cicero, are you the sixth vice-president of the
IBHT—?"

"I decline—"

"Mr. Cicero, are you and Mr. Joey Hopper the actual owners of a string of gas stations, a number of
trucking companies, and a racing stable, and have you
also used your union affiliation as a front for narcotics operations?"

"I decline—"

Brinkley: "Well, there were a good many other questions from Mr. Crawford. All of them different, and a
good many answers from Mr. Cicero, all of them the
same. Including the answer to Mr. Crawford's question—
"Mr. Cicero, is 'Cicero' your right name?"

There is reaction in the Nielsen living room.

Then David Brinkley introduces the highlights of
testimony by Cicero's eldest son, Vincent, Jr.

"In the two years since Joey Hopper was elected on
a reform platform," Crawford says, "Vincent Cicero, Jr.,
has realized commissions of more than three million dol-

*lars. There has been testimony here that Vincent Cicero,
Jr., was never in the insurance business before Joey
Hopper's election as president of the IBHT with the help
of Cicero delegates.*

*"There has been testimony from legitimate insurance
companies that their bids for coverage of the IBHT pension fund were from ten to fifteen percent lower than
young Mr. Cicero's bid. Cicero insurance companies have
consistently thwarted investigator Sal Santoro's efforts to
study their records—complicated records, because Vincent Cicero, Jr., has no fewer than twenty-seven different
insurance companies, and the cross-bookkeeping is a
maze, or maybe the word is a mess of financial double-
talk. Also, large sums in cash are missing, amounting to
more than $200,000. Did Vincent Cicero, Jr., turn this
sum over to Joey Hopper in return for the lucrative IBHT
multimillion-dollar pension business?"*

*Young Cicero, a nice-looking boy who never meant
to hurt anybody but only to make a buck, swallows hard
and turns to his counsel, "Governor" Thayne Winslow.
No constitutional fireworks, only the weary, self-
ashamed: "I decline to answer on the grounds that it may
tend to incriminate me."*

*The hearings go on—with sharp comments from
Chancellor-Brinkley.*

Art Nielsen and his family watch restively.

*Finally Joey Hopper takes the stand. The chairman,
Senator McAllen, reminds him that when Hopper first
took office he begged for time to clean out the criminal
influences in the IB himself. Now he has had the time.
What has he done?*

Joey Hopper gives the chairman his ever-more-practiced answer. He was given a list of 168 officers allegedly guilty of criminal activities. It is not a simple task to check them out. And constantly being harassed by this Committee is not making it any easier. Some of the men are up for trial, and the union has no right to interfere with judicial procedures. Some have paid their debt to society and he is one of those who believe in the American principle of rehabilitation. And still others are being judged by their own locals.

Crawford asks: "In other words, Mr. Hopper, in the case of these 168 officials of your union accused of criminal practices directed against the members of your union, you sit there and dare to tell us you have done absolutely nothing?"

"I'm handling it in my own way," Joey Hopper answers arrogantly.

"Mr. Hopper," Crawford says, "what you call 'your way,' including collusive arrangements with favored corporations and secret deals with known mobsters, Mafia lieutenants, and top traffickers in narcotics, could lead to the destruction of this Republic."

Thayne Winslow breaks in. "Mr. Chairman, my client is here to answer questions, which I believe he has done to the best of his memory and ability. The chief counsel is beyond his rights in making self-serving editorial statements."

Crawford slaps his papers down on the table and lowers his head to the mike. "Mr. Chairman, perhaps I cannot match the eloquence of the ex-Governor, but I truly believe I more than match him in ethics. I believe that he actually conspired with Joey Hopper, Allie Stotzer, and other key figures of the IBHT in the malicious destruction of legal papers subpoenaed by this Committee."

Chairman McAllen frowns at the chief counsel. "Mr. Crawford, this is a very serious charge. The only fair thing to do in Governor Winslow's behalf is to put him under oath and question him about this alleged conspiracy."

Thayne Winslow: "With all due respect for this honorable body of the Senior House of our great United States legislature, I must decline to answer on the grounds that my answer might tend to incriminate me."

Senator McAllen shakes his head. The list of Fifth-Amendment refugees now includes not only known criminals but supposedly respectable businessmen and politicians as well. One begins to fear that the business of any individual in America, if honestly described, might tend to incriminate him!

Dennis Crawford turns to the chairman. "Senator, in fairness to the workingmen and -women of this country, some fifteen million strong, organized under the banner of the AFL-CIO, I think we should remind our witnesses of the statement of its Executive Council: 'It is the policy of the AFL-CIO if a trade-union official decides to take the Fifth Amendment for his personal protection and to avoid scrutiny by proper legislative committees, law enforcement agencies, or other public bodies into alleged corruption on his part, he has no right to continue to hold office in his union.'"

The chairman says, "Thank you, Mr. Counsel. We

believe a powerful and honest transportation union can be a tremendous asset to our country. But since our last hearings I say with sorrow that Mr. Hopper has given aid and comfort not to the friends of labor, but to their enemies. Mr. Hopper loves to hold forth about his interest in the betterment of the workingman. What have we found him doing?—bringing in hoodlum extortionists, using union funds to grant multimillion-dollar loans to known leaders of organized crime, running the largest union in the country with all the democracy of a banana republic. These hearings are not over. We are not through with you, Mr. Hopper, or your underworld army. Is there no one—no one in your all-powerful organization of one and one-half million members who is willing to step forward and tell what used to be considered the simple truth?"

Art Nielsen and his family are listening to a wry comment by Brinkley on this heated exchange when the doorbell startles them. Art goes to the door cagily. It is a telegram. "From the Committee," he says quietly. "They want me there tomorrow afternoon."

Art stares at the wire in his hand. What should he

do? A family council forms around him spontaneously: Edna, Art's father, Sara Nielsen, and the newest member of Petroleum Drivers Local 101, Tommy.

"Well, here it is," Art says. "What do they call it in the bullfights—the moment of truth?"

"Don't go," Edna says. "Let's just say you never got it."

"They can check with Western Union. Anyway, that's not the way out. Do I talk or don't I, that's the problem."

"Art, I know you tried to follow out what Pinky started," Sara says. "But you've got a family to support, you've got yourself to think about."

"I agree with Sara," Edna says. "They'll get you up there and make you point a finger at Vincent Cicero and Tiny Lake and finally Joey Hopper—and Dennis Crawford will be a hero, and you—in a way Joey's right, do you think they really worry about you?"

"What do you think, Pop?" Art asks his father.

"In the old days I'd say sure, fight 'em, we was Wobblies, we believed in one big union that would finally take over this country and run it for the good of everybody. But now—Big Labor on one side, Big Business on the other, Big Government trying to run 'em both—so I got to go along with Edna and Sara: It's taking an awful chance—and the fight ain't worth it."

"They'll put a bomb under the house." Edna becomes more heated. "Or you'll step on the starter of the car and—bang! You know what they do. Art, I hate their guts just as much as you do—but why should it be *you?*

Let some single fella be a hero. You've got to think of the kids."

"I am. I'm trying to." Art struggles with himself, hopelessly torn. "I don't want to go down there and point fingers. I don't care about gangsters like Cicero and Lake —but Joey Hopper, I don't think Crawford knows how hard it is—even J. B. Archer I hate to hurt, I was getting to understand him. But Joey—to get up there under the lights and finger your oldest friend . . ."

Edna goes over and sits on the edge of his chair. "Art, I hate to ask you this. I know you never did a dishonest thing in your life. But if you have to go down there, don't answer the questions."

In a flat monotone, Art tries it on for size: "I decline to answer on the grounds that it may incrim . . ."

He puts his head in his hands. "And come back here marked a crook like the rest of the bums." He moans to himself, "Oh Jesus, Jesus Christ, Christ Jesus, help me!"

Edna says quietly, "He testified, and He got nailed to a cross, and we worship Him for it. But I'd rather have a live husband than a dead saint."

Art stares at his wife and gets an idea. "Look, we're an old democratic union family. Let's put it to a vote. All in favor of declining to answer . . . ?"

Edna raises her hand, then Sara, and finally, reluctantly, Grandpa Nielsen.

"All in favor of telling the truth?"

Tommy takes the floor. It's not easy for him to get started, but he's given this a lot more thought than he's admitted to anyone. "Shit, Uncle Art, I hate like hell to

go down that street. I'm not crazy about this Crawford
fella. Like Aunt Eddie says, it's easy for him to sit up
there on his high horse and tell us what to do. He doesn't
have to take the lumps. And if he hits the front page, it's
a big score for him on the way to whatever he's after—the
Senate, maybe even the White House. I sorta agree with
Joey Hopper on that. . . ."

"Then you agree with us?" his grandfather asks.

Tommy puts his right fist into his left palm and rubs
his knuckles slowly back and forth, a thoughtful variation
of Joey Hopper's belligerent trademark. "Uncle Art—I
guess—on this particular one—I vote for telling the truth."

There are murmurs of surprise.

"I hate like hell to cooperate with government—goes
against everything Grandpa taught me. And Pop. If we
can't make it with our own brains and our own muscle,
it's tough shit. We just gotta work harder."

Old Man Nielsen nods. "Unite the membership.
Build from within . . ."

"Trouble is, the Joey Hoppers and the Vinnie Ciceros got us by the balls. They've got it rigged so only the
officers vote at the Convention. And who appoints the
officers? Local democracy's a joke. Stand up 'n' talk, you
get a knuckle sandwich. Get up again 'n' they throw your
local into receivership 'n' run it from headquarters. You
gotta hand it to 'em. They got it down to a science."

They are all listening, hard. In front of their eyes,
Tommy Nielsen is growing up.

"If we had our own power base, our own protest
moving along, I'd tell Denny Crawford where to stick it.

I'd tell his Committee to stay the hell out of our war. But we don't have enough troops for a war yet. We're just a handful here, a handful there. What Uncle Art's got to say will put our message on TV all over the country. If we're ever going to have an honest-to-God labor union again—not a pork barrel for the Ciceros—this may be the time to use Denny Boy and *his* Mafia."

Tommy talks straight to his uncle, as if they were alone together.

"If you've lost your guts, Art—and who c'n blame you, you've taken plenty—we got some young guys in 101 who aren't buying this Hopper 'n' Cicero shit. The whole IB high command needs a good stiff kick in the ass. What you've seen, what you've got to say'll give 'em that kick. Then us Muscle Hollow kids—and the guys all around the country hurtin' just like we are—we'll try to keep on kickin'."

He pauses, takes a deep breath, and then blows it out like a distance runner at the finish line.

"End of speech. I vote for tellin' the truth."

Old Man Nielsen stares at his grandson, and then turns slowly to Art. "I change my vote."

"Then it's two to two, Art," Tommy says, beginning to take over this meeting. "The deciding vote is yours. What's it gonna be—?"

Art looks at his hands. He rises and paces. He studies the subpoena. He goes to the autographed picture of Joey Hopper in its place of honor over the television set: "To my oldest pal, keep pushin' for 101! Your union brother, Joey."

He is still staring at the picture when the phone rings. It's Dennis Crawford, in the Old Senate Office Building. The atmosphere there is hectic—investigators, witnesses, secretaries, clerks, all working furiously; Crawford has been at it all night. He apologizes to Art for telegraphing the subpoena without prior explanation. He had wanted to discuss it with Art personally, but there just wasn't time. Now he has to know where Art stands.

Art still hasn't made up his mind. He says he'll think it over on the flight to Washington. "It isn't as black-and-white for us as it is for you, Mr. Crawford," he says. "Even when you know they're wrong, it's hard to fink on your friends."

"Are you finking on them? Or are they finking on you?" There is silence on the other end of the phone. "Hello?"

"I'm still here," Art says.

"Well?"

"I told you—I'll think it over."

When Crawford says, "Okay, see you tomorrow," his tone conveys more feeling than he is able to express.

Tommy, as cold and tough as Joey Hopper but moving in another direction, has listened to the phone call. As soon as Art hangs up, he asks, "So?"

"Jesus, I wish I was a hero," Art cries. "On TV all you get is bad guys and heroes. Kojak. Columbo. I know some bad guys, but I don't know too many heroes, Tommy."

"Speeches," Tommy says.

"What did you say?"

"In five more years you'll be another J. B. Archer."

"You musn't talk to your uncle that way," his mother says.

"I'm a member of the IBHT," Tommy says. "I got a right to talk. I pay my fifteen bucks dues every month. I got all the rights I need."

The doorbell rings. Art starts toward it. "Be careful," Edna warns.

"Who is it?" Art asks through the door.

"Western Union," comes the answer. "From Washington."

"Maybe I don't have to go down tomorrow," Art says over his shoulder. He opens the door. Then he falls back, screaming. Two shadowy figures are running away. Art turns toward his family in agony, acid streaming down his face.

In Crawford's office the news of the assault on Art Nielsen brings everybody running.

Crawford feels a knot in his stomach. In a way it's his fault. He was pushing Art too hard. . . .

"Bullshit," Dave Edelman says. "You were asking him to come down and tell the truth. He was a valuable witness."

Crawford chokes back his sentimentality. "Hey, maybe we c'n get the FBI to get off their butts and nail the bastards who threw the stuff. Offer 'em immunity if they'll tell us who put out the contract."

"Joey Hopper and Vinnie Cicero," Phil Mahoney says.

"Right," Crawford nods. "Butch Cassidy and the Sundance Kid. Maybe this time they went too far."

48

---

*J*oey Hopper hurries into his home in Capital City, the same old $25,000 five-room frame, and before he knows what hits him, Paula is scratching at his face. By the time he can bring his guard up, she has made him bleed.

"What the hell, Paula? You gone nuts?"

"What you did to Art!" she screams. "I heard it on the radio. He's gonna be blind. He was getting ready to testify against you and you had your boys hit him with that horrible juice!"

She rips and tears at him. "Down, girl," he says. "I never said acid. Art's my oldest friend. You think I'd hit 'im like that, you're outa ya fuckin' mind."

"Monique told me," Paula cries. "You went to see him with Tiny and Bugsy and those other goons, and the next thing, he's blind. I love him, Joey. I guess you always knew it. I just couldn't say no to you—like everybody else—maybe that's why you did it."

"Number one, I didn't do nothin'," Joey says. "Sure I went to see him and asked him not to fink on the union. Hell, you're a labor broad, Paula. You know about stool pigeons."

"But you left him blind! Just like a criminal—like Vinnie Cicero. Every day more and more you're like Vinnie. Big labor leader! Hoodlum! Thief! Hoodlum!"

Joey knocks Paula down. It's a hard punch, bloodying her mouth, but born and raised in Muscle Hollow, she gets up, runs to the bathroom, and locks the door. Joey bangs against it. He can hear her at the medicine chest. He knows what she's trying to do. "Paula! Paula! Open the fuckin' door!"

"I won't, I won't," she gasps. "This time I'm going to do it. You won't have to worry about me any more."

With all his strength, he crashes against the door, smashing the lock. The door splinters open. Paula has just begun to take a handful of sleeping pills. Joey grabs her, forces her mouth open, smacks her on the back, and makes her spit them out.

"You're a helluva Catholic!" His fingers dig into her arms. "Takin' human life. It's as bad as murder."

"Don't talk to me about murder!" Screaming: "You gotta have your way in everything, don't you? You won't even let me kill myself in peace." She twists herself from his arms. "I wish I was dead! I wish I was dead . . ."

Joey says firmly, "You're not dead. You're Mrs. Joey

Hopper and you're gonna live. Ya hear that, Paula? That's
an order."

He grabs a towel and wipes her face with a little
more tenderness than one might expect from Joey
Hopper.

He leads her out of the bathroom. "I gotta run to a
meeting. If anybody calls, you don't know where I am."
He starts toward the door, then turns back quickly and
kisses her on the cheek. "I love ya, Paula. It's just that I'm
always in a hurry. Every five years or so remind me to
remind ya."

Paula stares after him.

49

At a late-night summit meeting in Joey's enormous
office are Thayne Winslow, Lou Vass, J. B. Archer, the
dapper Allie Stotzer, Vincent Cicero, and lesser officials
like Ned Green, Ace Huddicker, and others, including the
now-subdued Tiny Lake.

Pacing up and down, Joey dominates the meeting.
First of all he's furious because he never meant for them
to go that far with Art. Stammeringly, Tiny Lake tries to

defend himself. Regardless of physical size or position, everyone in this room is frightened to the tremble point by the sheer presence of Joey Hopper.

"Look, Joey, when I said a stronger dose, and you didn't say nuthin', I thought you meant . . ."

"Shut up!" Joey shouts. Tiny retreats, close to tears. "We've got to move on to the trial." He turns on Winslow. "I can see it in your fat, stupid face, Thayne. You're running scared." He grabs the once-dignified Governor by his lapels. "Maybe I never got through the sixth grade, but I'm a postgraduate at my own kind of law. Put an X-ray on that jury panel, Thayne. I wanna know the politics of every one of 'em, if they ever did time, how much money they got in the bank, who they sleep with, if they're white, chocolate, or polka-dot. And then, Allie, maybe you'd better make a pass at the judge. Damn few judges won't reach under the table for a little brown bag full of C-notes."

Lou Vass rises. "Governor Winslow, as of this moment I am resigning from your office and from this case. I'm as greedy as the next man, and I've had to defend a lot of things in the last two years that I was frankly ashamed to go home and tell my wife about—but I *am* a lawyer. I'd like to remain one. Good evening, gentlemen." He picks up his briefcase and heads for the door.

Joey chases him, ready to slug him, but Vass stops him with a quiet statement. "You can knock me down, Mr. Hopper, or have Mr. Lake work me over, but it isn't really necessary to your cause. According to our code, everything I heard here just now—no matter how shocking—was privileged and I would have no right to divulge it."

At the door, Vass turns to address his senior partner. "I hope I sleep a little better tonight, Governor. Ever since you got me into this, I've been living on Valium. I don't see how you sleep at all."

Joey Hopper wheels on the others as Vass exits. "I never trusted that four-eyed Jew-bastard. I had 'im marked for a fink the first time you brought 'im in, Thayne."

Knowing that Lou Vass has spoken a truth he will never be able to get his own mouth around, Winslow has nothing to say.

Undeflected, Joey continues to dictate the strategy. "So okay, we work the jury, we work the judge, and if worse comes to worse, Tiny, you say you did it, it didn't have nothin' to do with the union, just some personal matter, some bet Art welshed on. The most you can get is five years and you might even beat it on appeal, don't you think so, Thayne?"

The cowed Winslow says, "Possible, possible, Joey. We'll certainly try."

Tiny Lake makes his own appeal. "Joey, I'd certainly like to oblige, but I'm a two-time loser. One more and they're liable to sit me down for a long time. How about Bugsy Bender? He's got a pretty clean record. Six months for making book and another short stretch for pandering."

"Okay, Bugsy is a good idea," Joey decides. He turns

to Cicero. "Vinnie, you pass 'im the word. Tell 'im he'll get his regular salary from the local all the time he's away, and his job will be waitin' for him when he gets out."

J. B. Archer sighs. Tiny's huge face glows with relief.

The trial of Bugsy Bender for felonious assault against Art Nielsen is in many ways a rerun of the Senate Committee hearings.

Art Nielsen, his sightless eyes hidden behind dark glasses, tells the court that he had been under constant harassment from IBHT goons trying to discourage him from testifying against them. When he refused to make any promises, Joey Hopper came to see him. Joey warned him that he might get hurt if he went along with Dennis Crawford. The next thing he remembers is going to the door and—splash, the acid in his face.

Thayne Winslow, convincing in his role as a seeker after truth, asks Art if he was able to identify the men at the door. Art admits it all happened too fast for him to see their faces. Later he thought the one who called out "Western Union" sounded like Tiny Lake.

"Speculation," Winslow objects, and the judge, who seems to be leaning toward the defense, sustains his objection.

When Joey Hopper gets on the stand, he proves an effective witness in his own behalf. It's no accident that, as he crosses his legs, one of his shoes shows a hole in the sole. In establishing his home address, he also manages to get in the fact that he still lives in the same $25,000 house he first rented, then bought, on moving to Capital City. Of course, he came to see his old friend Art Nielsen in Hendersonville when he heard that Art was being harassed by Denny Crawford into testifying against the union. He never said that Art might be hurt—possibly Art misunderstood when he said that Art might hurt his original union convictions if he helped the Committee in its antilabor plot against the IBHT.

Joey speaks like a reasonable man, and the prosecutor is willing to accept his testimony at face value. Conspiracy is a can of worms; to try to pin the authorship of the crime on Hopper will only muddy his case. What the prosecutor needs to build up his record is a clean verdict of guilty on the assault charge. So he only goes through the motions in asking for conviction on all counts, including conspiracy.

Finally Bugsy Bender takes the stand. Bugsy readily admits that it was he who threw the acid. It didn't have nothin' to do with the union, he insists. Joey Hopper, Vincent Cicero, none of the IBHT big shots knew a thing about it. It was a private feud he'd been having with Art

Nielsen for a long time. Nielsen lost a two-thousand-dollar bet and when he welshed—well, Bugsy admits he was wrong, but that's the whole story of the acid.

The jury files in and the foreman breaks the tense silence to say that the defendant, Roland Bender, has been found guilty of felonious assault. But the jury did not feel that the prosecution proved its charges against Joey Hopper as an accomplice, or in any way involved in a conspiracy with Bender against Art Nielsen.

The jury's exoneration of Hopper evokes jubilation from his boys, an emotional "God bless the jury" from Tiny Lake, and exasperation from the Crawford team. Once again Joey Hopper has picked up all the marbles.

Leaving the courtroom, Art is being led by Edna on one side, Tommy on the other. To their amazement, Joey Hopper swaggers up to them.

"No hard feelin's, Artie," he says. "I know ya told the truth like ya saw it."

Art doesn't answer.

"Just t' show ya how I feel about ya," Joey goes on, never rebuffed by rebuff, "I want ya t' come back to the IB. Ya got a job with us f' life. Thirty G's a year an' all the fringes."

Art still doesn't answer. Nor does Edna. Tommy Nielsen glares at Joey. With him it's open hatred now.

"Well, think about it," Joey continues to grandstand. "My door is always open." Regally, surrounded by admirers, hangers-on, and frantic photographers, he sweeps out.

"Think about it!" Tommy shakes his head. "Some labor leader."

"We still have three kids to feed," Art says quietly as he makes his way to the street with Edna's help.

5¹

*F*rom his wide, top-floor window in the IBHT's monumental national headquarters, Joey Hopper is looking down at the fancy-tiled pathway around the reflecting pool that fronts the building. He is watching Art Nielsen, heading toward the entrance on Edna's arm.

Joey nods with satisfaction to Vincent Cicero and Tiny Lake. "One thing ya gotta say f' us—we look after our own." The elegant alumnus of the Apalachin Conference exchanges a smile with his oversize enforcer.

Enter Allie Stotzer, looking as usual as if he had just stepped out of a *Playboy* ad. He has laid out the program for the Joseph T. Hopper Testimonial Dinner. He wants Joey's okay before sending it to the printer. Proceeds are to go to the Joseph T. Hopper Home for Sightless Children, in Sunniland, California. That was J. B. Archer's idea—and a damn good one, Allie admits.

"Ya see, eggheads is valuable," Joey grins at Cicero. "Even if he does call ya dirty names like 'diner-saw.'"

The Testimonial Dinner is a triumph of Allie Stotzer's genius for American hype, with a liberal assist from J. B. Archer's ambidextrous idealism.

Aside from the distinguished gathering at the speakers' table, there are 175 extravagantly decorated tables, each seating 12 guests in black tie, at one hundred dollars per plate. Only in America could one find such a glittering, brilliant, and motley assemblage. There are the great heads of industry whose continuity of activities depends on the benevolence of Joseph T. Hopper, accompanied by wives competitively displaying their Halstons, their minks, their diamonds. There are university personages for intellectual window dressing—college presidents and celebrated economists—thanks to J. B. Archer's influence in those circles. There are priests, ministers, philanthropists, and social workers, attracted simply by the humanitarianism of this evening's cause: assistance to blind children. And of course there are tables presided over by prominent members of the syndicate, Vincent Cicero in a beautifully cut silk tuxedo, accompanied by his jewel-bedecked Monique. In the good taste of their dinner jackets, complete with cummerbunds and fancy pumps, Cicero's IBHT delegation is indistinguishable from the elegant array of two thousand other guests here to pay homage to General President Hopper.

An impressive front table just below the dais is hosted by a suave septuagenarian, Hiram Shecter. Originally from Chicago, a poor law-school graduate happy to

run errands for Mr. Capone, he is now the Henry Kis-
singer of the Miami-Las Vegas-Hollywood axis. He pre-
sides over his table of studio chieftains, movie stars, and
sequinned top-ten vocalists as if he were Louis XIV in a
midnight-blue tuxedo, graciously granting audience to
the most favored of his court. Beautiful women, some famous, some infamous, hurry over to plant chic, admiring
pecks on his tan and Chaneled cheek. The head of the
most active studio in Hollywood has described his good
friend Shecter as "the power behind the throne." Although there has been little personal contact between
them, since that is Hiram's style, Joey Hopper describes
Shecter more accurately: "The power behind the power."

Almost covering one large wall is an overpowering
photomural of Joey, flanked by smaller but still sizable
pictures of Joey's father, labeled (by Allie Stotzer)
"Labor Martyr," and an especially attractive photo of
Paula, taken when she was years younger, slenderer,
more beautiful: "Labor Wife."

Paula has a place of honor at the speakers' table. Expensively gowned, wearing a huge orchid corsage, she is
serving out her life sentence: the dutiful, doting wife of
the great labor leader.

Also at the long, flower-laden main table are Mr. and
Mrs. J. B. Archer, ex-Governor and Mrs. Thayne Winslow, Mr. and Mrs. Allie Stotzer, the president of the National Trucking Institute, and other important industrial
leaders. And to take this assembly full circle, there is also
the mob-dominated president of the Atlantic Longshoremen's Association, shoulder to shoulder with the militant
leader of the International Union of Pacific Longshore-

men—representing the two ideologically opposed maritime groups that Joey Hopper is working hard to bring together in the interest of "transportation unity."

An impressive benediction opens the proceedings. "Thou Who art our Ruler over all life, we Thy humble servants seek Thy forgiveness for our many sins . . . we ask Thy Divine mercy so that we may cleanse ourselves the better to serve Thee, our Lord and Saviour . . ."

Vinnie Cicero, and Junior the insurance expert, and Tiny Lake, and Three Fingers, and Harry the Horse, and Joey Hopper, and J. B. Archer, and Ned Green and Ace Huddicker—and Beverly Lambert, at a table discreetly near the main one—join other representatives of Big Labor, Big Business, and Big Crime in bowing their heads together in humble supplication.

The master of ceremonies is Miller H. Hansford, the ultrarespectable president of the National Trucking Institute. Representing the management side of the table, he says, he is proud to preside over this tribute to a great American, a great example of labor statesmanship, who by his diligence, patience, and integrity has contributed so much to the progress of this great American nation. . . .

At the speakers' table, Mrs. Hansford, who is susceptible to wine, confides to the wife of Mr. Hansford's legal aide that Mr. Hansford hates Mr. Hopper's guts but they've got to live in the same world, so how could he refuse Allie's request that he serve as emcee? "Shhhh," her friend warns her sharply.

Then Thayne Winslow is at the podium. In his long career as state senator, congressman, and finally chief ex-

ecutive of a great commonwealth—he warms up in sten-
torian tones—it has been his privilege to meet many great
Americans. But the man who has impressed him most of
all, including even some Presidents of the United States
he has been privileged to call by their first names, is the
man he is humbly proud to call his friend, Joseph T.
Hopper! Here is a man, the keynote speaker intones, who
works twenty-four hours a day to better the conditions of
his fellow workers. Here is a man who, under constant
government harassment, never once chose to take the
Fifth Amendment. And yet here is a man who never hesi-
tated to fight the good constitutional fight for his union
brothers—whether guilty or innocent—to avail themselves
of the privilege that was written into the Bill of Rights
for profoundly patriotic reasons by our Founding Fathers!
"Ladies and gentlemen, I give you one of God's noble-
men—Joseph T. Hopper . . . !"

The pandemonium recalls the moment of Joey's
nomination at the Los Angeles Convention years earlier,
when Art Nielsen was his ardent supporter and friend.
Nearly all the two thousand guests rise and applaud
while the band, this time a society band, plays "For He's
a Jolly Good Fellow. . . ."

It is some time before Joey Hopper, mounting the
podium before a bank of TV cameras, can quiet the demonstration. Almost the entire gathering is on its feet ap-
plauding to the rhythm of "He's a Jolly Good Fellow."
But pointedly keeping his seat at one obscure table, Local
101's, is Tommy Nielsen, now in his early twenties and already a union officer; with him are benign, aging Deac
Johnson, barrel-bodied old Porky Porcovich, the tough,

now thirty-year-old Billy Kasco—charter members with Joey and Art of the original Petroleum Drivers Local 1. This group is the only one in the great flag-bedecked auditorium which has not risen to join in noisy homage to Thayne Winslow's version of "God's nobleman."

While the Stotzer-inspired "Jolly Good Fellow" production goes on, it is being monitored nationally by interested viewers. In the AFL-CIO's Washington headquarters, leaders like George Meany, Douglas Fraser of the UAW, and others watch in disgust. In the Old Senate Office Building, the investigation team is also watching. Dennis Crawford chews on a pencil, Charley Walker compulsively makes notes, Dave Edelman puffs the stub of a cigar, and Phil Mahoney taps his pipe. Sal Santoro wipes his glasses and shakes his head, thinking of the thousands of financial statements, the telltale check endorsements, and bank withdrawals that make a mockery of The Joey Hopper Show.

Joey opens with a sentimental gambit, a moment of silence for a great friend of both management and labor, who did so much to help his fellowman and paid for it with his life as a martyr to the persecution of the Dennis Crawford Senate-protected "posse": George Henderson the Third. Then smoothly he segues to humor. "No matter what Denny Crawford says, forgive me, my friends, if I don't look as ritzy as our distinguished master of ceremonies or the Honorable Governor Thayne Winslow. I'm not much of a black-tie man, as my one million seven hundred 'n' fifty thousand boys c'n tell ya. When I heard you was goin' t' throw this little fish fry for me, I had t' go out an' rent this monkey suit."

When he raises his muscular right arm, the tight jacket rips at the armpit. "Sorry about that!"

Every effective demogogue has the timing of a stand-up comedian, and Joey Hopper brings down the house. "I didn't come here tonight to make a speech. You'll hear enough of them when Denny Boy's investigation of our International Brotherhood gets under way again." Again, he gets his laugh. "I don't say the last couple of years haven't been tough. I've been smeared, as Sam Gompers was smeared, as John L. Lewis and Phil Murray were smeared—I been smeared not only by Denny Boy Crawford and his Northeast Mounties galloping off in all directions, I've even been smeared—and as a workin' stiff it breaks my heart to say it—by the AFL-CIO, by the actual labor movement that oughta be standin' up for us instead o' makin' us out like pareeahs—" He looks down at J. B. Archer. "Right, J.B.?"

"Pariahs," J.B. corrects him, more or less on cue. "Ya see," Joey Hopper picks it up, "J.B. is a brain. So I let him write these here speeches for me. Only I cross 'im up—like I like t' cross up Denny Crawford an' the high 'n' mighty AFL-CIO—by changin' my answers t' fit the needs of my members as I go along. . . ."

In front of the various TV sets—in the homes of AFL-CIO officers and rank-and-filers, at the Crawfords', at the Investigating Committee's—there is a shaking of heads, a grinding of teeth, a near-unanimous feeling of *"Oh, what a devious sonuvabitch. . . ."*

"And now," Joey goes on, "without further ado, I want to thank all of you from the House of Labor, the House of Management, the House of Education, from the Judiciary and the Legislature, for honoring me tonight. J. B. Archer, our venerable Third Vice-President—I like to call 'im that because he's been thirty-nine for the last twenty years just like Jack Benny—anyway, J.B. informs me that the proceeds from tonight's occasion total—are you ready fer this?—come to two hundred 'n' forty-nine thousand, nine hundred 'n' ninety-seven dollars 'n' seven cents!"

Thunderous applause. Joey looks down toward the beauty-parlor mask of Paula, with apparent love. "Paula honey, if ya got two bucks an' ninety-three cents in ya purse, get it up and we c'n make it an even two hundred 'n' fifty thousand dollars, a cool quarter of a million, for the Joey Hopper Home for Sightless Children in Sunni-land, California."

Laughter and cheers rock the hall. And now Joey Hopper produces his hole card: "And what could be more appropriate than to turn over our two hundred and fifty thousand dollars to Brother Arthur Nielsen, to deposit for us in California—Brother Nielsen, who has suffered the slings and arrows of militant labor misfortune . . ."

Using a cane now, Art Nielsen comes in from the wings on the wave of another ovation. Nobody claps harder than Tiny Lake and Three Fingers Jones and Harry the Horse Mingus, beginning to sweat through their ruffled shirt fronts. Vincent Cicero applauds politely, as befits his higher rank. A distinguished *capo* several rungs above Cicero cries, "Bravo! Bravo!"

In the face of this glittering assemblage, Art Nielsen looks shattered; not just his sight but his old spirit and strength have been beaten out of him.

As he is about to accept the check from the smiling Joey Hopper, a striking resemblance to the great photomural grinning down at the banqueters, all of a sudden the shit hits the fan! A voice shouts out, "Don't be a patsy, Uncle Art!"

It's Tommy, who's run up and grabbed the mike. He talks a mile a minute, knowing he has to make his pitch before the pistoleros go into action. So Tommy's challenge quickly develops into a slugfest between the Tiny Lakes and the old Muscle Hollow loyalists, Porky, Deac, Billy, and the rest of them trying to protect Tommy's precious air time.

Despite the punch-shove-shout all around him, Tommy manages to say: "I'm Tommy Nielsen. I just got elected secretary of Petroleum Drivers Local 101, the outfit that grew out of my old man's death when I was a kid. I just want you to know our first order of business was to take a vote on pulling out of the IBHT—an' it was 1141 to 26! Eleven hundred and forty-one honest working stiffs to Vinnie Cicero's twenty-six jukebox clowns." Pulled away from the mike, Tommy fights his way back to it, a tough little quarterback defended by the 101 blockers as the opposing line tries to sack him.

"We call ourselves ROLL—Return Our Labor Liberties. We're asking the other locals in our Council—not the phonies Hopper let Cicero set up—to follow our lead. Back to trade unionism—the real thing! No more thieves spending our dues on diamond rings and trips to the Bahamas with their 'secretaries.' No more hoods throwing us down the stairs if we dare even show up at the meetings. We hate to say it because he was one of our own but Joey Hopper is a thousand times worse'n Bill Reed—he's turning the biggest union in the world into the biggest rip-off in labor history!"

Tiny Lake reaches over Deac's shoulder and belts Tommy on the jaw. But Tommy hangs on.

"Listen, the rest of you guys too scared t' talk back because you figure they'll hit you like they did Uncle Art, wake up before it's too late, wake up 'n' fight back, like we're starting to!"

There is more scuffling, shouting, slugging. With the help of his own broadbacks, Tommy manages to shout, "Join ROLL! Cut bait! Go straight! Let's ROLL!" Then he goes down, as the IB goons surge in.

Joey Hopper, Thayne Winslow, Allie Stotzer, J. B. Archer, Vincent Cicero, and a few others of the inner circle rush from the hall to their waiting Cadillacs. They'd better haul ass to the office and get to work. This is just one lousy little local out of a thousand, but it's got to be fought; a good strong statement from Joey for the press—immediately putting other Henderson County locals into receivership to choke off a vote, before the rebellion has a chance to spread. Maybe a smear campaign against this snot-nose Tommy Nielsen as a Commie . . . "I never did trust that punk kid," Joey snarls as he slams into his car and speeds off to his Taj Mahal. "I never liked the way he looked at me. . . ."

Dennis Crawford's suite in the Old Senate Office Building explodes in jubilation. This is one of the breaks they've been hoping for. Maybe their avalanche of facts is beginning to make an impact on the membership! Of course, this is only one small local, Crawford reminds them. Under the heel of Joey Hopper there are still a thousand, run from the top down by crooked officers who jump at his command. And Hopper is moving—like a Huey Long of the labor movement—toward his One Big Transportation Union: Everything that rolls, that sails, that flies is going to belong to Joey Hopper! That's what *he* thinks!

Jacket off, collar open, sleeves rolled up, Crawford goes back to work. From his window he looks across the park to IBHT headquarters. He sees all the lights on the top floor begin to flash on. "There they go—back to their homework!"

They have plenty of new areas to explore before the hearings open again. That California land deal that looks like a six-million-dollar steal; Joey making full-time organizers out of habitual criminals the same day they're sprung from prison; his special contracts with favored employers, worth countless millions to his cronies, Sal's come across three more that are beauties; his criminal partnerships with Cicero and other Apalachin alumni; the grand-larceny case against Cicero's son for the Health and Welfare insurance racket, *that* one they ought to be able to make stick! They—he and the rest of the investigating staff—aren't finished. But, looking at those lights on across the park, they'll have to dig deeper, work even harder. . . .

5²

---◆---

*I*t is almost a year later and a new administration has squeaked into the White House by a 1 percent plurality. As usual, the President has run on a platform of Compassion, Decency, Harmony among the races, Welfare Reform, Tax Reform, a Realistic National Budget, and Peace with our potential adversaries. His program is as soothing as his tone. Somehow the Republic has survived the turbulent sixties and the blizzard of hundred-dollar bills that snowed the country into the mid-seventies.

No one knows much about the new President, which is one of the main reasons he is elected. A fed-up electorate knows too much about all the politicians they are asked to support. A new face is welcome. A new broom to sweep clean.

The New Broom goes in for a lot of old-buddy ap-

pointments, but his eyes are so blue and his voice so sincere that one feels like a cynic for doubting him. Give
him a chance. At least he's trying. At least he is not
shackled by party-machine politics, or indebted to the
Eastern Establishment, or to the Big Business alliance
that has dominated the preceding administrations.

Like all politicians, old face or new, he is an accomplished tightrope walker. With a soft smile on his face
and a sweet song in his heart, he could probably walk
across Niagara Falls on a high wire. Or without one.

So along with the usual down-home appointments,
he makes one surprising one. His Attorney General is
Senator Justin McAllen, who not only has a national reputation but helped swing the border states. McAllen in
turn appoints as his Deputy Attorney General in charge
of the Criminal Division—Dennis Crawford.

The Crawford appointment finds Joey Hopper outdoing himself in four- and six-letter words. "That snotty
little cocksucker! Before, it was just a lot o' garbage at
the hearings. Now he thinks he's positioned himself
where he c'n do something about it. Because I was born
poor an' he was born rich, he's on a goddam hate kick. I
never trusted nobody who didn't work himself up from
the bottom. Those fuckin' bleedin' hearts make me vomit.
Denny Boy thinks he c'n nail me with a lotta canceled
checks, illegal wiretaps, and some fink witnesses who've
got shit in their hearts? Over my dead body!"

Crawford has brought his old team—Walker, Santoro, Edelman, and Mahoney—into the Justice Department, but now the little army has been reinforced by
twenty lawyers and investigators, working with agents of

the IRS and the FBI, an around-the-clock strike force
that Joey calls the "Hopper Posse." Even some of the
deep thinkers of the Washington and New York press
wonder in print if Attorney General McAllen isn't permit-
ting his scrappy little organized-crime fighter to indulge
his personal vendetta against Hopper at the expense of
other criminal activities.

Crawford lets none of this sniping, whether from the
press or from Hopper and his friends in high places, dis-
tract him from his goal. He's putting in eighteen-hour
days and whipping the large, able staff to follow suit. Jan
worries about him. When he even lets his squash game
get rusty, to her that's a sure sign that his Hopper obses-
sion is affecting his health.

In vain, Crawford tries to explain to friends and enemies alike that his campaign to "get Hopper" is not a personal vendetta. It is simply that his intensive study of
IBHT activities over the years has convinced him that
"Joey Hopper is the sewer through which the mob flows
into the labor movement. And once they get control of
the largest labor union in the country—and the big trucking companies prefer the mob to legitimate union leaders
as the lesser of two evils—you can forget the President's
faith in 'restoring traditional values.'" Those values are
going down the drain, along with the country that's better at preaching than putting them into practice.

Crawford is working now not on open-ended hearings but on evidential indictments. The Agerts Oil case
looks like a winner. Even if Paula and Monique refuse to
testify, they've got enough documentation to prove that
Joey and Vincent Cicero set up their own trucking com-

pany, with industry support, and paid their drivers two dollars an hour less than the area contract Joey himself had negotiated. Then there's the Sunniland Retirement Development outside Palm Springs, California. Hopper and his friends—not only Cicero but two of Vinnie's superiors in the organization, the brothers Al and Tony Figliuzzi—have reached into the pension till for two million dollars, deposited it in a Palm Springs bank *without* interest, and in return received a loan on easy terms to build split-level retirement houses they are offering to aging truckers at twice their actual cost. Horatio Alger took too long. The Brothers Figliuzzi are becoming multimillionaires overnight.

There are so many juicy cases to choose from that Crawford urges his staff to be selective. Pick the ones surest of conviction, and also calculated to arouse the membership that's still inclined to shrug at Joey's wrongdoing so long as they have meat on the table and a decent pension at the end of the line.

There is one case so extreme that Crawford thinks Santoro has mistakenly added three extra o's, when this Sam Spade of accountants reports that Allie Stotzer has borrowed *sixty-two million dollars* from the IBHT Pension Fund without even the formality of posting collateral, and with that union largesse bought three different casino hotels in Las Vegas. Stotzer in turn has sold a controlling interest in these gambling palaces to Hopper and Benny the Bat Batinelli, the Sun Belt lieutenant for the Genovese family. An interesting footnote is that the lawyer who handled the complicated legal machinery—a real paper chase—is Hiram Shecter, who operates from his hideaway ranch outside Scottsdale, Arizona.

All very enlightening, says the red-eyed Crawford, but is it strong enough for indictment? Will it stand up in court and convince a jury? Sure, Walker has wiretapped incriminating phone conversations between Joey and Benny the Bat.

"But those wiretaps are illegal," Crawford points out. "Helpful. But illegal."

"We're also working on a hit man in the Batinelli organization who made the mistake of getting caught, and who's ready to talk if we drop Murder One to Murder Two, and set him up after parole with a new identity."

"Make any deal you have to," Crawford says. "Who cares about the little guys? We've got to nail Hopper and his godfathers at the top."

While the Hopper Posse presses on, Tommy Nielsen and his ROLL recruiters manage to pick up seven thousand members around the country. Seven thousand out of two million may sound like a handful of minnows trying to stand up to a school of sharks. But the rebels are encouraged. For every member with the guts to join openly —and face the leg-breakers—there are ten more who know they're on the short end but have to live with it. ROLL newsletters are showing up on the bulletin boards of locals from Bangor to San Diego. They don't stay up long, but as quickly as they're ripped off by the cowboys, they mysteriously reappear.

Tommy tries to gauge the secret resentment against the sewer rats crawling all over the International. Not that he has any illusions of overnight change. In fact, from a hospital bed where he's recovering from an ambush that left him with fractured ribs, Tommy tells a local reporter he's not sure they can ever lop off enough tentacles to kill the octopus. "But if you quit," he says through broken teeth, "you die."

53

The Agerts Oil indictment makes the front page. On the network evening news, Dennis Crawford says this is only the first of a series of indictments that he is sending down with full confidence that Hopper will be found guilty by a jury of his peers. "This is the first step in the long march," Crawford says. "In our opinion there is now an excellent chance that the reign of terror and wholesale exploitation of the IBHT is coming to an end."

Watching this announcement on the large TV set in his office, Joey Hopper laughs out loud. So okay, this is more serious than all that shit in the hearings. But nobody fucks with Hopper and lives. Not that he plans to knock off that little sonuvabitch, he assures J. B. Archer, who is now his First Vice-President. He won't have to. He'll just run him around in so many legal circles that the kid will hit the canvas like a punched-out fighter.

He picks up the phone. "Get me Lee Bailey, honey," and bangs it down again. "Thayne Winslow has the right look for the hearings. But he ain't smart enough for Denny Boy. Lee will give him all he c'n handle."

He sees the worried look on Archer's face and tries to cheer him up. "Don't gimme that fuckin' do-good frown. Go out an' have a nice three-hour lunch. With a head-job f' dessert. I promise, they won't lay a glove on us. Hopper is here to stay. And so are you, *and* Vinnie and the boys. Let's face it, J.B., I need the both of yuz. That's the way it works!"

J.B. does exactly what Joey advises him to do, has a five-martini lunch at the Sans Souci, and winds up with Beverly Lambert back at the suite in the Madison for which the union lays out five thousand a month, not including room service. She's worried about his responses. When she first became his personal secretary, all she had to do was touch it. Now it's taking him longer and longer. "Too much vod," she scolds. "And worries," he adds quietly as he reaches down and runs his hand over her blonde-rinsed hair.

Hiram Shecter's ranch retreat in Scottsdale is a thousand acres of irrigated desert land, rich in date palms, camellias, hibiscus, and bougainvillea. The home itself, a ranch house of palatial proportions, is at the end of a winding driveway a third of a mile from the high, electrified fence. A guard is posted at the gatehouse, and the security of the lord of this desert castle is maintained by the latest innovations in electronics, plus armed guards with revolvers and attack dogs at the ready.

Night has fallen and Hi Shecter has finished dinner with his wife and eldest daughter home from Stanford for the weekend. She is an A student excited about her new course in the philosophy of religion. Shecter suggests a new book on the subject that even she hasn't heard about, and that has just been reviewed at exhaustive length by an Oxford professor in *The New York Review of Books.* Shecter is a rare-book collector. But unlike some of his Hollywood friends, he doesn't collect them just for show. As a first-generation newsboy in Chicago, he had inherited from his immigrant failure of a father an insatiable love of books. His hunger for quick money had led him to the action, and in his early twenties he already had been as hooked on wealth and what it could provide him as less resourceful street kids are on smack. He loves to look at his beautifully bound books, and sometimes when he is alone in his library with its sliding walnut ladder to the balconied second tier, he enjoys picking out a book at random, *Bleak House* or *Vanity Fair* or *Life on the Mississippi,* and losing himself in the familiar text wherever he happens to open it.

Over the years he has developed exquisite tastes. He has his share of Cézannes and Renoirs and a drawing he bought from Picasso himself, when he was in Monte Carlo visiting his dear friends Prince Rainier and Princess Grace, to whose charities he is a liberal contributor. In all of his houses, from Jupiter Beach in Florida to Acapulco, he has paintings worth fortunes. There is a Rothko that is a special favorite and in the library an explosive Debuffet he bought early for a fraction of its present value.

His Chinese butler mutters something to him and he

excuses himself to go into the den. There, just arrived by small private jet from the La Costa Country Club north of San Diego, are Paul Figliuzzi, the lawyer in the Figliuzzi family, Vincent Cicero, Jr., the insurance tycoon, Allie Stotzer, and Jack Odoms, whom Shecter respects both because he has a computer-quick legal mind and because he has been for the past twenty years a trusted friend of Meyer Lansky and Moe Dalitz. Shecter and Odoms speak the same language, class and cash.

Young Cicero is impressed with the place, the collection of cars in the driveway, from Rolls to Mercedes-Benz, the stables, the putting green, the gymnasium with the obligatory sauna and Jacuzzi, the sixty-foot swimming pool in the shape of an S, with a waterfall and a rustic bridge arching over it, the flower gardens all lit up at night. . . .

"Nice place you got here, Mr. Shecter."

Hiram nods, and lights his meerschaum. "Thank you. It's comfortable." The butler pours cognac in large snifters, then discreetly withdraws. The host democratically offers cigars, Upmanns. Even though they've lost the casinos there, they still get them from Cuba. There is a pause, and then like a Chairman of the Board, Hiram Shecter gets down to business:

"I've done everything I can with my friends in Washington. I even reminded an old friend fairly high on the White House staff that I was one of a dozen people the President had a private dinner with out here when he was still a candidate looking for substantial contributions to his campaign."

He puffs portentously on his pipe. His audience waits respectfully.

"But I'm afraid the time isn't right. A year or two ago it might have been different. We had more clout with the other administration. Not that I see us in any great danger in the long run, but for right now I'd have to say there's nothing we can do for Mr. Hopper."

Stotzer protests, politely. He knows Denny Crawford has a "Get Hopper" complex and can't be swayed. But he had been hoping Hiram could use his influence to get to McAllen, who may not be corruptible but at least is open to reason, and persuade him that going all the way with these indictments—including scores of them against other IB officials—could disrupt the party and upset an economy already shaky and threatening to the President's future.

"The trouble is, this problem suffers from overexposure," Shecter explains, like a professor of political science instructing his class. "Crawford and Joey have locked themselves into a power struggle. One has to lose for the other to win. Crawford's rep is on the line. So is Joey's. My job is working out compromises. Switching tracks to avoid head-on collisions. But you all know Joey. He'd rather fight than switch. I'd like to see some plea bargaining. A light sentence and early parole. But with Joey's ego, no way. He'll pay Lee Bailey, or rather he'll get the IB to pay Bailey, to fight it all the way to the Supreme Court. That won't do any of us any good."

Paul Figliuzzi looks at young Cicero, and Junior stares at his hands nervously.

Shecter continues, in his quiet, professorial tone.
"The Joey Hopper trial will keep the IB on the front page
for months, maybe years. It will lead to further indictments. There'll be newspaper exposés, books. Important
people who don't like to see their names in the paper will
be held up to public scrutiny. That's bad for business.
And we're not talking about millions any more, but bil-
lions. When you deal in that kind of money, you want a
low profile. Joey has brought in a million new members,
and he's structured the organization so there's no way to
get rid of him, unless it's something really drastic. . . ."
He lets the underspoken phrase float slowly over them
like an invisible storm cloud—and then, in the same mat-
ter-of-fact voice, continues: "And of course none of our
friends want that, if it can be avoided."

"What if he calls the national strike he threatens to if
he's arraigned?" Jack Odoms asks. "To stop everything
that moves in America. God knows, he's got the guts and
the charisma to do it."

"Exactly," Shecter says, able to talk with the mouth-
piece of his pipe clenched tightly in his teeth. "But
there's such a thing as too much guts and too much charisma. 'One giant transportation union that can cripple
this country!' That kind of threat scares everybody, from
the President down to the welfare mother. The trouble
with Joey is, even with all the money pouring in, he
never quite outgrew that militant kid on the picket line.
Somewhere in his blood he still hangs on to the One Big
Union idea. My clients have too much at stake to be jeop-

ardized by the rhetoric of an egomaniac. Let's leave Superman to the movies. He's expendable."

The final word comes down on his listeners like a sharp blade. Paul Figliuzzi nods and starts to rise, a signal for the others to follow. "Thanks, Hi. I can see you've given this problem a lot of thought. We'll fly back to La Costa and see what we can work out."

Shecter sees them to the door of the den, which has a private entrance from the driveway, where a chauffeur-bodyguard is waiting to drive them back to the airport.

"I'm sure your friends will know how to handle it," Shecter says, with a little bow.

As Shecter moves through the den to rejoin his family, his private phone rings. It's Teddy Mack, of Olympia Records, one of the biggies in the rock field. They're having trouble with the hot new group that's beginning to gain on the Bee Gees—Tom Swift and the Swifties. Tom (whose straight name is Arnold Axelrod) is flying on ego and coke, has a new girl and a new personal manager, and wants to split from the group, pull out of his movie, cancel the Sands gig, and go to India for a month of meditation. And then the punk threatens to take a year off to campaign for the nomination of his political idol, Jerry Brown. That little whim, Teddy Mack figures, could cost Olympia ten million dollars, not counting the lawsuits. It's worth a hundred thousand to Mack and his partners (who are rolling in laundered money) if Hiram could straighten this crazy kid out.

Shecter says he'll be happy to talk to Tom when he

sees him at the Heart Fund Dinner he's cosponsoring in Beverly Hills next week with Dean Martin, Debbie Reynolds, and Frank Sinatra. Hiram may be able to drop a few names that will bring "Tom Swift" into line. It should be worth 10 percent of Olympia's potential take on the package, payable to Shecter's law firm. Then he goes to the family room, which is decorated with various humanitarian plaques and framed photos of himself with a score of national celebrities, from Nixon and Bob Hope to Jimmy Connors and Joey Hopper, and settles down to watch a PBS broadcast of *Tosca* from the Met.

In the $250,000 Figliuzzi home overlooking the golf course at the La Costa Country Club, Paul and young Cicero report back next morning to the Figliuzzi brothers and Vincent Cicero. When the word "expendable" is translated, Vinnie tries to stick up for his old pal and partner. Not that anyone mentions Joey Hopper by name. They all know the shorthand that leaves no tracks, just as Hi Shecter described "the problem" in language calculated to protect him against ever being nailed for having handed down the sentence. Now Vinnie is told that since he is closer to the problem than anybody in the organization, he's obviously the one best qualified to take care of it. Let Vinnie handle it in his own way. Like Shecter, the Figliuzzis have a lot of other things on their mind. They'll read about it in the papers. Then they go out to play in the Invitational Golf Tournament, along with some of the leading pros in the country, to help raise funds for J. B. Archer's Summer Camp program. Vinnie has a five handicap and loves the game but he decides to cancel out of the tournament. He pours himself a stiff drink instead. He'll have to pour a lot of them before this is over.

54

$\mathcal{J}$oey Hopper is out on $50,000 bail, taking a rare week off, lying low at the summer cabin he built with his own hands on a pond about twenty miles from Capital City. Paula is with him but she's not much company and he's lonely and bored when he's out of action. He's not too worried about the Agerts case because Lee Bailey is pretty sure he can get a hung jury. Rolling up behind it, like ocean waves, is the Sunniland case. But the finances on that one are so complicated, deals within deals and wheels within wheels, that it should be easy to get delays, and when they finally go into court it will be a battle of accountants with so many figures flying around that a jury of the simpleminded may never understand it. Meanwhile, against the advice of the more cautious heads in the union, Joey has been keeping up a barrage against the "power-hungry and vengeful Denny Crawford." He thinks he can drill that image into the minds of prospective jurors and that at the end of the road he'll come out on top and Denny will be tripped up on his way to the Senate.

When the phone rings it makes a startling sound in the cabin because Joey has just had his private number changed for the third time in three weeks and only his lawyer and his intimates have the latest. His voice rises with the old verve when he hears who's on the other end. "Vinnie baby!! I missed you, kid. How they hangin'?"

He's missed him, too, Vinnie says. He's on his way out to see the new country place he's just bought and is renovating. He has to pass Hopper's joint on the way. He thought maybe Joey'd like to take a load off his mind and see it with him.

"You got it, baby!" Joey says. "I'm goin' stir-crazy in here. Paula's drinkin' is drivin' me up the wall. I been shootin' little birds from the front porch to keep from goin' off my rocker."

Vinnie tells him, to save time, to meet him at the Big Mim's Diner at the corner of Highway 25 and Pond Road. In exactly thirty minutes.

Joey tells Paula he'll be back in a couple of hours and gets to the diner a few minutes ahead of time. Vinnie arrives a few minutes late. With him are Tiny Lake, Harry the Horse, and Champ Cristoli, all old friends. Joey's spirits are on the rise. It reminds him of a lot of battles they rode off to together—and won! As they will again!

Since they now have two cars, Joey suggests that Vinnie drive with him, while the boys can follow behind.

Vinnie is a little surprised that Joey doesn't have a driver, especially now when he's under pressure.

"Fuck pressure," Joey says. "I never liked chauffeurs. Let J.B. and all the other vice-presidents have their chauffeurs. I like to drive. Gives me somethin' t' do."

"They tell me Denny Crawford drives a convertible himself. With all his money. All that government juice."

"Fuck his money. Fuck the government. We got enough money 'n' juice to beat his ass."

As they drive farther into the country, through the changing foliage of October, they talk about more pleasant things. Their heavyweight, Georgie Gardner, is ranked Number Six now, and if he wins the fight coming up in San Juan, they could line him up for a title shot and some really big bucks. And their little filly, Betsydear, has just won her first stakes for fillies and mares and looks ready to go a mile against the boys.

"It's been a lot of work," Joey says. "I guess it's time we had a little fun."

Vinnie looks over at Joey in surprise. In all their years together, he's never heard him say that before. It's always been go-go-go. Joey never learned how to play. Like golf. Even with their own country club, and that beautiful twenty-seven-hole course, he never even tried the game. But there's something about him you've got to respect. Vinnie admits it, he looks up to Joey Hopper. He's worked and fought for everything he's got, he deserves to be running the show. Too bad he got himself so far out on a limb. Vinnie would have liked to be pals with Joey all his life, but it just wasn't in the cards. Cicero is a big man in his own woods, pulling down a quarter of a million a year and all he can steal—but in the bigger jungle around him there are animals that can swallow him alive.

A few miles down the road they come to a high, imposing gate, through which they can see a road leading to a lake. It's the latest of J. B. Archer's dream places, the newest IBHT summer camp being readied now for next June. Archer is going to play host here to a thousand boys and girls from union families all over the state. And, on the other side of the lake, there's to be a vacation camp for senior members, named for Franklin Delano Roosevelt, still Archer's idol.

"Hey, I got an idea, le's go in and take a look," Vinnie suggests.

"That J.B.," Joey shakes his head. "He's still a New Dealer at heart. Maybe a socialist. He never quits. A real bleedin' heart. But I'll say one thing for him, we got the best social benefits in the country. That don't do us no harm."

They get out of the car, open the gate, and look around the grounds. The recreation center. The campsites. The tennis courts. "An' wait till you see the pool," Vinnie says. "A big wadin' pool for the little kids, an' just beyond it an Olympic-size for the Tarzans."

Joey goes over for a better look at it. It is still only an enormous hole in the ground, with thick wire netting shaping it to hold the cement that will be blown against it by a Gunite machine.

Vinnie stands alongside Joey as he stares into the deep end. "Nice little hole ya got there," Joey says. "Looks like a grave for King Kong."

Vinnie doesn't smile because out of the corner of his one eye he sees Tiny Lake coming up behind Joey with a section of lead pipe used for shower-room plumbing. Holding it in his two big hands like a giant baseball bat, Tiny smashes it down on Joey's head. The sound of pipe on skull is terrible, and blood begins pouring from Joey's head. But he doesn't go down and he doesn't topple over the edge of the hold. Instead he wheels on Tiny. "Motherfucker!" he screams. Again Tiny hits him with all his might, this time in the front of the face, smashing nose and cheekbones.

Joey's features are masked in blood now. "Motherfucker!" he screams again and moves toward Tiny. Tiny takes a step back and looks to Vinnie for help. Joey's voice is strangled in blood. "C'mon, mo'fo'ker . . . !" The gory head with the dented skull keeps moving toward Tiny. "Jesus, Mary, 'n' Joseph," Tiny sobs. "How d'ya kill this sonuvabitch?"

What is left of Joey Hopper lurches toward Tiny Lake. There are fat beads of perspiration on Tiny's face. They had decided on clubbing instead of bullets because sound travels far in the country and gunfire might attract attention. But who would have thought a man could stand up to Tiny Lake and a lead pipe? Joey should have gone down with the first blow and died with the second.

"Mo'fu . . . !" The bloodied beast is still reeling forward. Terrified, Tiny raises the pipe again and this time Joey reaches out and tries to close with him and wrest the pipe away. But just then Harry the Horse, almost as big as Tiny, with the shoulders and chest of a wrestler and the bulging, muscular belly of an old cop on the take, hits

Joey over the head from behind with another length of pipe. They can see the blood well up through the hair like red water from an underground sprinkling system. Now Joey goes down, still moaning "Mo . . ." Tiny stares down at him in awe and fear: *What if this bastard is some kind of a god, who will get up even now and take them all down with him?*

"Jesus, Mary, 'n' Joseph," he blubbers. "Eats lead pipes like it's candy."

"Still breathin'," Champ Cristoli says, and kicks the body over the edge into the deep end.

While Tiny turns away and Vinnie watches, trying to keep a hard face on it but feeling puke in his belly, Champ and Harry the Horse jump down after Joey. There's an opening in the wire netting, and beneath it a specially prepared trough that's waiting for Joey. They roll him into it, then fasten the netting over him. They know about cement. They had been hod carriers who worked their way up in the Cicero Cement Company. Cement is a very nice business. Sidewalks and sewers. Cosa Nostra, Our Thing, has you coming and going.

Champ crawls up out of the hole and switches on the Gunite machine. In the deep end Harry the Horse holds the large hose as the Gunite begins to flow from the nozzle. He aims the stream at the bloody, inert, but still breathing body which will lie cemented there forever under the meshing that lines the pool where youngsters will frolic next summer.

"I'm sick," Tiny says. "I need a belt bad." His face is bathed in sweat. Vinnie notices that Tiny's big hands are trembling. *He's too fat,* Vinnie is thinking. *He's got a big*

*heart but he's got fat in his heart. Chicken fat. Champ
and Harry won't give but Tiny could be a problem. Life
would be simpler if there were no more Tiny.* Vinnie gets
into Tiny's car, after telling him to lose Joey's, and drives
out through the gate. He feels bad about Joey but he's
grown up in this business and he knows you have to do a
lot of things you don't want to do. And swallow it down
where it leaves a lump in your stomach. That's what sep-
arates the real tough from the Tiny Lake tough.

That night Vinnie takes Monique out to the new
disco he has a piece of, takes her home, and screws her so
fiercely she thinks it's their second honeymoon.

55

$\mathcal{T}$he disappearance of Joey Hopper sparks big headlines. It makes Art Nielsen say, "I knew it. I knew it.
They play too rough. Even for Joey."

Tommy Nielsen puts out a ROLL Extra. This isn't
going to make reform any easier. Joey Hopper had become a monster but at least he was something you could
aim at, like Henderson in the old days. But now it turns
out he's just a small monster swallowed up by bigger
monsters. Monsters without names or faces. The La Costa

Country Club monsters. Who's gonna testify against *them?* The fact that Joey Hopper is gone only proves that the IB's real bosses are more dangerous then ever. If they can hit Number One and get away with it—as he knows they will, they always do—then there is no protection, no law, and no justice. The fuzz is pretty good at picking up the punks for street crime. But white-collar crime and organization hits, the cops don't even bother with, same as the FBI—they both know they're licked before they start. Tommy and his die-hards in ROLL aren't kidding themselves. They've got one little finger in the dike and the tide is rising over the dam. But the motto still goes: "If you quit, you die."

In his office in the Justice Department Dennis Crawford takes it just as hard. He feels almost as if Joey Hopper has cheated him out of that conviction, he was after him so long. Crawford wanted Hopper behind bars, not crushed between smashed cars in a cemetery of rusted metal, or wherever they put him away for good. All of Crawford's old teammates feel the same way, as do most members of the new task force. The FBI can bulldoze and excavate the country from coast to coast, and a thousand to one they'll never unearth the remains of Joey Hopper. You've got to hand it to the boys who terminated him; from a purely professional point of view, they are masters of their art. If the perfect crime means never getting caught, the Genoveses, the Gambinos, and the Figliuzzis, working through their Vinnie Ciceros, make perfect crimes an everyday affair.

Crawford even has a file on Hiram Shecter. But he's never been arrested, and he never will be. He's a lawyer, so his conferences with clients are privileged, sacrosanct. And he has friends in such high places that you take your political life in your hands if you even dare to question him.

"So what do we do for an encore?" Charley Walker asks. He's ready to quit and go to work for the NAACP. "We're grinding our wheels in the sand. At least when I played tight end for Dartmouth I got to catch a touch-down pass once in a while. Here I feel as if I keep running the fanciest patterns I can and the quarterback has to keep eating the ball."

Sal Santoro agrees. Since he's been on this job he's had to buy two sets of stronger eyeglasses. Now the lenses are so thick, they frighten his little girl. "All we've succeeded in doing," Santoro says, "is set up Joey Hopper for the hit—and throw the rascals *in* instead of out."

Crawford tries to hide his own discouragement. They've got a fistful of indictments, from the Brooklyn and Jersey mobs to the raids on the Central States Pension Fund, the highway robberies of Las Vegas, and the multimillion-dollar shenanigans of La Costa. Chances are, three out of four will be acquitted; they may get a Cicero or a Benny the Bat for commercial bribery or income-tax evasion, but—face facts—they'll never get them for what they really did. There is no murder in the Joey Hopper case because first you've got to find the body, and that's like looking for a needle in the deep Pacific. He doesn't blame Walker or Santoro for quitting, but the rest of them have to keep on spinning their wheels, even if they have to spin ever faster just to stay in the same place.

A few weeks later there's more bad news. Tiny Lake's been gunned down outside a topless joint on the outskirts of Capital City. The gunsels just shot him at point-blank range and drove away. Nobody saw anything, of course. No license plate. Just shadows that drove away.

Champ Cristoli, Harry the Horse Mingus, and Three Fingers Jones are working a Meyer Lansky casino in the Caribbean. Vincent Cicero has been promoted to third vice-president of the IBHT. And the new International General President is J. B. Archer. A smart move: He gives the outfit credibility, a link with the good old days of social progress. And he's in so deep he couldn't clean up the union if he wanted to. Archer will always hate the dinosaurs, but he caved in to reality a long time back. He's *persona grata* at the White House now. He represents millions of votes and a stream of hundred-dollar bills that flow into Democratic as well as Republican coffers.

Crawford is not too surprised when Attorney General McAllen calls him in to say they have to cut back the Hopper Posse at least by half. The removal of Joey has taken a lot of the "sex appeal" out of the operation. McAllen is under pressure not to put all of Justice's eggs in one basket; many other areas merit looking into. McAllen would be the first to appreciate and commend Crawford's zeal in keeping after the IB racketeers. But they don't have a monopoly on crime and corruption in this country.

The Attorney General isn't exactly ordering Crawford to call off the dogs, but Dennis gets the message. A new election is coming up. The President's record isn't quite as pure as pictured when he was a brand-new face on the national political scene. To win this time, he'll need a lot of key industrial states where the IB has clout. Better to bend now and live to fight another day.

Jan Crawford knows Dennis so well that she can read his mood by the way he gets out of his car and walks to the house. By the halfhearted way he rough-houses with the kids who run out to greet him. By the way, after his customary two wind-down martinis, he pours himself a third. Dennis isn't a serious drinker, but about twice a year he eases himself into a frustration drunk.

"Well, Jan, I think I've had it," he says when they've said their prolonged good nights to the children after dinner and are sitting together on the small couch in the den, facing the fireplace. "I think I've run this ball about as far as I can carry it. I can't seem to convince anybody, not even my boss, that I didn't have it in for Hopper, I had it in for Hopperism, and that it's stronger today than ever. Before, it was like fighting a dragon. Now it's like fighting a hydra with a hundred heads. So we lop off two or three and they do a little time, like Carlo Gambino, with all the power and all the money right where they left it, growing bigger every day."

As he pours another drink, Jan tries to reassure him. "At least you slow them down, put a little fear into them."

"I don't believe that any more," Crawford says. There is a long pause. "I think it's time to throw in the towel. Hand in my resignation."

Jan looks at him. "It will be New Year's Eve from Miami to La Costa."

Crawford shakes his head. "For the Figliuzzis and the Ciceros and the Hi Shecters, every day is New Year's Eve."

"I refuse to believe that."

"My loving little patriot. You want me to keep pushing that stone up the mountainside like Prometheus?"

"Sisyphus."

"Sisyphus, right. Prometheus was chained to the mountain. I feel like both of 'em." He reaches for the pitcher.

"What you're going to feel like in the morning is another question."

"I think I'll call in sick in the morning."

"You've never done that before."

"Take a long walk in the woods. Clear my head."

"What would you do if you quit?" Jan has begun to take him seriously.

"Take six months off to think. Not just about us. The country, I mean. No more white hats and black hats. Those jokers know what they're doing. Black hats with white trim. White hats with black bands. Or should I say 'green'? Three cheers for the red, white, and green. They're putting dollar signs where the stars used to be."

"Are you running for office?"

"On the platform, I'll wind up dogcatcher."

"Or dead," Jan says.

56

*N*ext morning, Dennis Crawford, back from a three-mile walk through the frozen woods, impulsively picks up the phone and calls Tommy Nielsen.

"Hi, Tommy. Denny Crawford. How's it going?"

"Still in one piece," Tommy says guardedly.

"I wonder if ROLL could use a good lawyer? Have shingle, will travel."

"Hey. Are you serious?"

"Maybe you've got the right idea. Fight 'em from where you're coming from. Justice, the Department, is running out of gas."

"Wow. You're *serious!*"

"I'm going through the want ads. Thought I'd try you first."

Tommy Nielsen is silent a moment. A moment too long.

"Denny, I appreciate this. A hell of a lot. A big step down from the Justice Department to workin' for peanuts for ROLL. But . . . I don't know how it'll go down with the fellas. We're strictly rank and file. We got our own lawyers who are members of the IB. We don't want to look like—"

Another pause. *If we had our own protest moving, I'd tell Denny where to stick it. Tell him to stay the hell out of our war. Even if hit men did a job on Uncle Art, that still doesn't make him a hero to my guys. They want to kick ass on their own, not through the Uncle Arts, forever marked lousy as Government stools. And now if we let Crawford sign on with us, J.B. and his limos will know how to get the mileage out of that to piece us off from a lot of rank-'n'-filers who oughta be with us.*

Crawford chews on a thumbnail and speaks into the silence. "Okay, okay. I get the picture. Lots of luck to you."

"Thanks. We're gonna need it." And then: "So will you."

"Thanks, Tommy. Let's stay in touch."

Dennis Crawford sits there, a long time. Then, after Jan hurries the kids off to school, he tells her he's feeling a little better, he guesses he'll go to the office after all. Keep pushing that stone up the mountain. Three cheers for the red, white, and green. As a contemporary philosopher, Satchel Paige, put it, "Don't look back, they may be gainin' on us." Or, as Tommy Nielsen says, "If you quit, you die."

Power tends to corrupt and
absolute power corrupts absolutely.
                    —Lord Acton, 1887

Power sucks.
                    —Graffito on wall of
            Manhattan subway station at
                Ninety-sixth Street, 1979